A Traveler's Guide to Living

What six years spent as a visitor on Earth taught me about being human

By Dupont Rockefeller Jackalone, Jr.

www.atravelersguidetoliving.com

This book is dedicated to the lost

...wherever they may find themselves.

Cover illustrations by Eric Tirado

Technical and moral support by Michelle Steward

Looking

Prologue 1.0

I'm not an explorer.

Technically, I'm on vacation. I left my planet six years ago to pick up a case of bourbon and a few boxes of cigars on Earth.

Then I lost my can.

That's how my adventure started – with a team of community activists cleaning up a vacant lot. Looking back, it's hard for me to believe. But it's as true as water is wet.

Let me tell you my tale and what I've learned since I was marooned. I can guarantee you've never heard anything like it before. And you'll never hear anything like it again, even if you live as long as we Paladinos do.

I have to warn you, though. If you're a fan of science fiction hoping to hear about extraterrestrials flying UFOs around outer space, you'll be disappointed.

This is a story about ordinary humans living right here on Earth.

It's my story.

And there's nothing scientific or fictional about it.

Prologue 1.5

You'll be glad to know that I'm going to talk in English. Most of the words translate OK. The ones that don't – like jrhkdibn – will be pretty obvious.

Speaking English is fun. It's full of alliteration and analogies and metaphors and similes and idiomatic expressions and all sorts of figures of speech that make a conversation sound like a musical composition.

My original language, Phonetic Alphanumeric Lingo, which we call PAL, is as plain as vanilla ice cream. It's also very complicated and full of rules.

Like #227. Roughly translated, it says: Two Letters with Hanging Tails Can't Appear in the Same Word Unless Separated by a Z.

If you had the same rule, a baby buggy would be a baby bugzgzy. And a simple word like goop would be gzoop or gozop or even goozp.

These days, I'd rather speak Pig Latin than PAL.

Prologue 1.75

I was 27 Earth years old the day I decided to make a long-distance trip to buy supplies for the mating season on Paladin.

Under normal circumstances it's a snap – an easy-as-pie, six-step process that I'd successfully completed a dozen times before:

1.) Vaporize into my travel can.
2.) Whiz 12.5 million miles through the universe to Mulberry Street in Newark, New Jersey.
3.) Re-solidify into the form of a human.
4.) Pay the clerk at Bifano's Grocers & Liquors for my booty.
5.) Stop for a piece of cheesecake at Henry's Café.
6.) Re-vaporize into the can and arrive home in time for dinner.

New Jersey, home sweet home
by Dr. J.J.

What could be simpler?

But this day was different. People who say practice makes perfect just don't know how factors outside your control can mess up your routine.

Heck, can change your life.

I'm proof of that.

And it's all because a bunch of do-gooders picked up my travel can and tossed it in a Dumpster.

Yes, the first five steps went off like clockwork, as they had on every other trip.

It was the sixth step that was the problem.

Someone stole my ride, and I've been trapped in Jersey ever since.

Chapter 1
An intergalactic shopper arrives in America

I had lingered over my cheesecake that day, watching the server play some kind of game on a cell phone and checking out the *Newark Star-Ledger*. I flipped through the front section, stopping at a headline that puzzled me:

DNA test reveals gender 8 months before birth; bioethicists worried

The article by Peggy Crowley went on to explain that a new blood test enables expectant parents to find out the sex of their baby-to-be as early as five weeks into the pregnancy.

I continued reading, confused but curious:

> The Baby Gender Mentor kit includes two pregnancy tests and envelopes for collecting and sending a finger-prick blood sample to a Massachusetts laboratory. The lab charges $250 for processing and e-mails the confidential results within 48 hours.
>
> Because embryonic DNA is present in maternal blood, the sample is tested for the presence of the Y chromosome, which indicates a male. If there is no Y chromosome, the embryo is female. The test does not need FDA approval because it is not used as a diagnostic tool.
>
> While surveys of Americans show no general gender preference, some cultures prize boys far above girls. That preference is fueling trends in India and China, for example, in which the number of boys born each year outstrips girls beyond the natural ratio of about 105 males to every 100 females.

I didn't understand a single word of the newspaper story. On Paladin, it simply doesn't matter. All Paladinos are zibizzibiz, which roughly translates into English as femans. Males and females act alike, think alike and look alike.

I shook my head in disbelief. I would have to be blind not to notice that males and females on Earth look different. In fact, on all my visits I had felt an unusual interest in the curvy creatures who had bumps on their behinds *and* lumps on their fronts. Because Paladinos are always looking for shortcuts – in speech as well as travel – I thought of them as Blumps.

But the newspaper article implied that Earth men and women don't just *look* different, they truly *are* different. And that because of those differences, some families would actually prefer a boy to a girl, and vice versa.

I pondered the meaning of the story for almost an hour. I turned the newspaper upside down and right-side left, hoping I'd gain a clue about the significance of sex selection. Twice the server refilled my coffee cup and twice I slurped it dry, hoping for a flash of insight.

Finally I gave up.

I wanted to get back to Paladin. Back to a place where gender had no importance anywhere – except in a Station for Elemental Xerographic Replication of Organic Material (SEX RoOM). Otherwise known as a procreation laboratory.

I picked up my shopping bags and walked out the door of Henry's. For the first time since I had started traveling to Earth more than seven years ago, I felt like what I was – an alien.

A stranger in a strange land filled with strange creatures with strange notions.

I couldn't wait to get home.

I hurried back to the vacant lot where I had landed. In a few minutes I'd be on my way to Paladin, where everyone is like everyone else.

As I said, it was almost the mating season, so I'd soon be called on to serve my time in a SEX RoOM. I didn't look forward to the assignment ahead of me. I didn't dread it. It was a job, something all of us 20- to 60-year-olds had to do.

At least I'd be in a world that made sense. And I'd have some good bourbon and cigars to enjoy when my duties were over.

I looked around for my travel can. The area where I'd touched down wasn't large – about the size of a tennis court – so I could tell right away that it was cleaner than it had been when I arrived.

Gone were the paper bags, Styrofoam cups, and broken bottles. No more airless basketballs, church bulletins or plastic six-pack holders. Not even a filthy wad of dried-out chewing gum.

Everything had been cleared out and carted off.

Everything.

Including my travel can.

This was no ordinary can. In fact, it wasn't really a can at all. It was actually a Cosmic Accelerator and Neural Neutralizer (CANN).

It allowed us Paladinos to vaporize, journey through the universe, re-solidify into the same form as the beings where we landed, then vaporize again for the journey home.

Don't ask me how it worked because I can't tell you. Not because it's a secret. I can't tell you because I didn't understand then and I don't understand now.

Truth is, I never cared. The engineering behind my CANN mattered to me about as much as the science behind an exercise wheel matters to a hamster.

Give me the when and where. Let someone else – like maybe the scientists at NASA – deal with the how.

CANNs are as common on Paladin as bicycles are in China. We were eligible to buy one at age 20, and most Paladinos spent their birthdays waiting in line at the agency where they were sold.

CANNs were expensive, but the purchase price covered lifetime ownership, as well as computerized maps of Designated Travel Territories (DTTs).

I'd heard rumors about hard-core travel addicts who recovered only by returning their CANNs to the manufacturer. But I was skeptical. Turning in a CANN meant being grounded forever. The owner could never get another one.

That's why I didn't believe the rumors. Paladinos are the most-traveled creatures in the universe. It's what we do. The mere thought of being stuck at home for eternity gave us claustrophobia and hives.

Voluntarily give up a CANN? No chance.

Not even if the addiction caused financial ruin, carpal travel syndrome, or bunions.

We took our CANNs for granted, the way people do things that were around when they were born and will be around after they die. Like paper clips or kite string.

To me, my CANN wasn't a "mysterious masterpiece of technological wizardry," as that awestruck reporter called it last month. It was a round-trip ticket to anywhere and everywhere in the globasphere I wanted to visit. Period.

All I had to do was say the name of my destination out loud, press the remote activator button, and away I'd go.

Touchdown automatically triggered the re-solidifying process, so by the time I "came to," I was standing on the landing strip, looking exactly like the people on the planet I was visiting.

When I was ready to go home, I pushed the remote activator button again, said "Paladin," and zoomed back through the stars.

One, two, three – as easy as A, B, C. That's all I knew. And like I told you, it's all I wanted to know.

Well, actually, there is one thing I've wondered about over the years, but it's not about the CANN per se.

I'd like to know whether anyone ever saw me appear out of absolutely nowhere.

Have you noticed those "You can see me but I can't see you" stickers on 18-wheelers barreling down the turnpike? It's the same idea.

Maybe people had witnessed my arrival without my knowing.

I don't really think so, though. I never heard anyone scream or saw anyone run away. Which sound to me like two downright sensible reactions to the sight of an alien coming out of a can in the corner of a deserted playground or parking lot.

But I can't be sure.

The experts who invented the CANN conveniently made the remote activator button smaller than a dime. I kept mine in my pocket at all times in case I was bitten by the travel bug.

Which happened frequently.

In the last six months alone, I'd racked up almost 17 billion miles on my Peregrinating Paladino account.

In case you're wondering, that's way above the average of 11 billion.

The CANN itself looked like a regular, Earth-type container, only larger. Not the size of a typical Hormel Chili can, or a Campbell's Soup can. If that's what you're thinking, think bigger.

Think Costco-sized.

It was bright blue, 15 inches across, 17 inches high and could hold the equivalent of 10 gallons of liquid. Who on Earth – or anywhere else, for that matter – could eat that much Dinty Moore beef stew?

Mine looked as if it had been kicked around the block a few times, and letters on the outside identified it as a brake fluid container.

Paladinos can't choose the CANNs they want. They're assigned. Nacho cheese cans, V-8 juice cans, pork 'n' beans cans – you name it, a Paladino's flying it.

The type of CANN we traveled in never changed, but the language on the outside did. For example, when I landed on Veknam in the Redix Galaxy, "brake fluid" or its planetary equivalent automatically

---

The truth about alien spacecraft

Most aliens prefer to travel solo. That way they have more flexibility regarding where they go, when they depart, and how long they stay. Paladinos fly in CANNs. Durbit vessels look like fist-sized rocks. Nordille zip around in the smallest mode of transportation: grains of sand. Restaxaneli, who live on an ice-cold planet and avoid all destinations with temperatures above 30 degrees, prefer snowflakes. You've heard the saying that no two snowflakes are alike? Restaxaneli have a real thing about being different – not only from other life forms, but also from each other. The next time you see snow flurries, I guarantee they'll contain at least one Restaxanelo coming to Earth for a refreshing winter vacation.

appeared on my CANN in the Veknam alphabet. How did it happen? It's another one of those "don't ask me"s.

All I can tell you is that Paladinos – especially Paladino scientists – are known for their superior intelligence. Relative to inhabitants of most other planets.

In my opinion, my CANN was the very best. Every time I used it, I smiled at the irony of hurtling through space in a brake fluid container. There was absolutely no stopping a Cosmic Accelerator and Neural Neutralizer.

No reverse. No gears. And certainly no brakes. Nothing but pure speed.

On my first several visits to Earth, I took the CANN with me to Bifano's and to Henry's.

A slice of heaven: Henry's cheesecake
by Dr. J.J.

Of course. As the scouts had said, it was my lifeline. A sure-fire guarantee that I could get back to Paladin whenever I was ready.

But three trips ago, a group of Blumps told me I couldn't bring a can of brake fluid into a restaurant, full or empty. They twisted their faces into funny shapes, pulled their small creatures close, and said they'd call the police if I didn't leave right away.

What would you have done?

Exactly.

I went straight back to the vacant lot that day, skipping my usual coffee and cheesecake.

An alien in handcuffs? Not this alien.

After that, I decided to leave my CANN behind for the 30 minutes it took me to shop and eat. I'd never seen anyone working or playing on the lot. It was full of all sorts of rubbish. I figured an empty brake fluid container wouldn't catch anyone's attention or interest. And, up until this very visit, it hadn't.

I glanced around the lot once more, hoping to catch a familiar shape in my peripheral vision.

Nothing.

I set down my bags of bourbon and cigars and methodically scoured the area.

Back and forth. Side to side.

No one can hunt like a Paladino. We learn advanced techniques through programs administered by the Chancellor of Exploration, Search and Trans-galactic Recovery.

We refer to the Chancellor as CHESTER, no matter what the actual name of the person in the office is. And CHESTER would have been very pleased with the thoroughness of my search.

But I didn't need X-ray vision to see that my CANN wasn't there. A big blue container labeled "brake fluid" would be hard to miss. Especially on a lot that had practically been swept clean.

So there I stood, a once-preening Paladino, stranded in a foreign land.

A few uneventful voyages to and from Earth had lulled me into a false sense of security. Millions of Paladinos had traveled before me, but I had believed I was the only one capable of successfully breaking the Inviolable Rule of Cosmic Trekking:

Never leave your CANN.

Why, even loud and proud Newark natives would have laughed at my arrogance.

Because of a few pushy Blumps at Henry's Café, I had put my fear of being identified as an extraterrestrial over what years of training had drilled into my head. Three times before, I'd been lucky. But today my luck had run out.

The scouts on Paladino, who were the first to venture into new galaxies and universes, had warned of such a possibility. Some travelers, they said, never return home because they don't want to. Others, they cautioned, never return home because they can't.

Because they lose their CANNs.

In either case, missing travelers who were found by CHESTER's office faced severe penalties and punishment.

According to Legislative Act 76, Section 9, Codicil 14, otherwise known as LASCO 76.9.14, *"It shall be illegal to create opportunities, occasions or openings for residents of other planets – in known or as-yet undiscovered universes, galaxies or solar systems – to disassemble, dissect or otherwise destroy a.) a Paladino CANN, or b.) a Paladino cadaver or carcass for the purpose of scientific investigation and/or possible replication of said commercial or corporeal property."*

Paladinos are required to follow the Keep It Short and Simple Regulation (KISSeR) when writing or talking. But not legislators. As you can tell, they have no use for KISSeR.

That's OK. Traveling Paladinos got the message loud and clear anyhow.

"You CANN't leave your CANN, you CANN't leave your CANN, you CANN't leave your CANN."

Over and over the scouts would make us say it, sing it, shout it and swear it at travel camp. Until it became a constant and, frankly, very annoying hum in our heads.

The scouts taught us to read, write and speak in the languages of our destination planet. Told us the best products to buy there. Trained us to blend into our environment. And, if we planned to visit for more than a few hours, they indoctrinated us on the people and cultures we would encounter.

But nothing we learned at camp was as important as, "You CANN't leave your CANN."

The mantra made perfect sense to me, and I'd lived by it for seven years. But after the scare I'd had at Henry's, I knew I either had to break The Rule or quit traveling to Earth.

You're probably thinking right now, "Why didn't you just go somewhere else to shop?"

It's a very good question. Here's the answer:

Petitions for changes in Designated Travel Territories are never, ever approved by CHESTER. I know plenty of people who have tried. There are simply too many roving Paladinos – 28.3 billion by last estimate – to let us go wherever we want.

Why, we'd be landing right on top of each other!

My DTT on Earth was Newark, specifically Vector 207.439.81888. I couldn't go to Tampa, Havana, London or Damascus. I couldn't even go to Trenton.

If I wanted bourbon and cigars, it was Newark or nowhere. And if I wanted the creamiest, tastiest cheesecake in town, I had to go to Henry's. Believe me, it's the best.

Because I traveled to Earth for food, not fun, I never stayed in the city more than 30 minutes. Stop, shop and go . . . that's the way I operated.

Besides, I didn't really like Newark. It was full of people with big hair, big personalities and big mouths.

But I did appreciate what the city gave me:

Slow, satisfying draws on a toasted Padron Anniversario Superiore Maduro that produced a cloud of thick, white tendrils around my face and enfolded my nose in an aromatic bouquet.

Deep gulps of Pappy Van Winkle's Family Reserve Bourbon that relaxed every fiber in my body as it flowed down my throat in a sweet and spicy blaze.

That doesn't sound like something I'd say, does it? You're absolutely right. I'm a pretty average Paladino, and as I told you before, KISSeR doesn't accommodate flowery words and sentences.

But when I left the SEX RoOM each year and retreated to the balcony of my apartment, looking out over the craters as I savored a cigar and sipped a glass of bourbon, I felt like a warrior-poet.

After a good smoke and a swallow, I could do or say anything I pleased.

Give up my supply missions? Impossible. I looked forward to – even depended on – rewards for my annual service.

Being in a procreation lab isn't exactly hard work, but it isn't fun, either. Hour after hour, day after day, and week after week spent in a series of chambers with other Paladinos participating in the xerographic replication process – some donating sparks and others donating seeds.

And you can't tell which is which because each and every one of them could be your mirror image.

Does the word "monotonous" pop into your head? Well, it doesn't even begin to capture the tedium of a month as a spark donor. As far as I was concerned, bourbon and cigars were my hard-earned payment for making new Paladinos. And I wasn't about to start working for free.

"I CANN leave my CANN. I CANN leave my CANN" became my new prayer.

I recited it until I believed that leaving my CANN at the landing site was a perfectly safe alternative to being hassled by angry earthlings, put behind bars and, ultimately, cut into pieces and pickled in formaldehyde for scientific study.

I believed it.

And then I did it.

But the sterile lot in front of me was iron-clad evidence: I was wrong and the scouts were right.

I thought hard about my predicament and swallowed even harder.

Then, right out of the clear blue, it came to me. The solution to my problem was so straightforward, I slapped my palm against the side of my head in amazement.

Ask someone where the trash had been taken. Go to that place. Retrieve my CANN. And zip back to Paladin.

Puddle of water
by Dr. J.J.

Once I was back home, I'd swear off booze and cigars, purge the word "Earth" from my memory, and plan a nice vacation to some other galaxy.

I *could* do it. And I *would*.

But I definitely needed more air in my system to succeed. Interacting with earthlings would consume all my energy. I had to look, act and talk like one of them.

The talking would be the most difficult. I never spoke more than a few words of English during all my trips to New Jersey. So I was afraid I'd sound like someone from another planet.

Which, of course, I was.

My blood, my body and my brain needed oxygen for the challenge ahead.

I had to soak my gills.

Just as I said those words to myself, the sky opened up and dumped a torrent of water that turned the street beside me into a shallow, litter-filled river.

Within seconds I was soaking wet, hair plastered against my scalp and shirt sagging over my belt.

Hooray! Could there have been a more positive omen? I chuckled with delight as I headed toward a puddle that had formed in a low spot in the dirt. It was time to get my feet wet.

As I walked, I looked around carefully, scrutinizing my surroundings as if my life depended on it. What I was about to do could land me on a laboratory table, dead, naked and prepped for dissection by scientists. Parts and pieces of me could end up in jars, on display in a biologist's office or on a museum shelf.

The truth about extraterrestrials

Aliens aren't little green men. Most aren't little. Fstwps, for example, are all over 55 feet tall. And I've never met a Mitherwit shorter than twice my height, which, on Earth, is six foot three. On the other hand, Balqs are about as big as a piece of lint. They live on the tiniest planet in the universe, and there wouldn't be room for more than a few hundred of them otherwise. With respect to color, aliens tend to be bland – kind of a gray eggshell. And 99 percent are genderless. Sexual identity is necessary only in the absence of science. When life is created in labs, chemistry occurs between molecules in test tubes, not between men and women in bedrooms, bars, or backseats. What do Paladinos look like? I don't want to spoil any picture you might have conjured up in your imagination. But in all due modesty, we're considered some of the most attractive creatures in the cosmos. Here on Earth people tell me I'm a dead ringer for . . . well, for a very famous – and handsome – sports celebrity. I'll let you guess who that might be.

But I had no choice.

Seeing no one anywhere, I loosened the straps on my sandals. I stared at my feet, which were covered with a dingy pair of slouching white cotton socks, and wiggled my toes.

Then I did it. I stepped right into the puddle.

Ahhhh.

I could feel the oxygen begin coursing through my system. What no one knew – at Bifano's or Henry's or anywhere else in the entire universe except Paladin – was that underneath each of my stretched-out casual crews was a set of gills that covered the entire instep.

Webster's Dictionary defines gills as "slightly green filamentous structures of vascular membranes." There's no way the people at Webster's could have ever looked under a Paladino's socks, but they managed to get the description right anyhow.

Earthlings would be shocked and even horrified if they saw my uncovered feet. But they don't know what they're missing. Gills are great. When they're wet, they help you breathe better.

In every other regard, I looked pretty much like a typical American.

My clothes were slightly frayed and out-of-style, but that was my fault. The magical inner workings of my travel CANN only took care of my physical shape and features. Following the local dress code was my responsibility.

After my first successful round-trip to Earth, I didn't want to jinx or put a hex on myself by changing into something more fashionable. Anyhow, my clothing didn't concern me too much. Newark was chock full of all kinds of crazy creatures dressed in all kinds of crazy costumes.

No, it was the whole combination of circumstances that had me worried.

I'd be in the worst kind of trouble if people became suspicious of someone in an outdated outfit standing ankle-deep in the middle of a puddle in a vacant lot during a driving thunderstorm.

That could lead to only one thing – being hauled to One of Those Places, where Someone in Authority would force me to take off my socks.

Revealing my gills would lead to loud screaming and widespread fainting. Which would lead to government agents being called. Which would lead to my being taken to a laboratory for further study.

I don't have to describe what would happen next, because I already have.

I told myself to *STOP*. I needed to quit thinking about what could go wrong and find out where my CANN had been taken.

I bent over to pick up my shopping bags, but they had been shredded by the rain.

Useless.

I couldn't possibly carry everything in my arms. I had no choice but to leave the bourbon and cigars behind.

Sounds familiar, doesn't it?

I know. But what else could I do?

I'll tell you what I *wanted* to do.

I wanted to break the seal on a bottle of bourbon, find a dry pack of matches under the cigar boxes, and enjoy myself until the warrior-poet showed up to help.

I might have done it, too. Except it was raining.

So I took an armload of my treasures over to the only possible camouflage on the lot – a scraggly bush in the far corner. After the last bottle and box had been pushed under the spiky branches, I stood up and hoped for the best.

Same as always.

Then I put on my sandals, threw my shoulders back in a show of determination, and walked toward Mulberry Street.

Along the way, I practiced a New Jersey accent.

Chapter 2
Stuck in place

Before I get to what happened on Mulberry Street, let me tell you what you've probably figured out already.

I didn't find my CANN.

Not on that rainy afternoon.

Not ever.

But not because I didn't try.

I looked high, low, and every place in between. California, Florida, Alabama, and Alaska. Morocco, Mexico, Haiti and Honduras. China, Ireland, Brazil and Botswana.

I traveled by motorboat, sailboat, cruise ship and dinghy. By bus, car, airplane, and freight train.

I saw oil cans, garbage cans, diaper cans and film cans. In Paris and Palermo I even saw a can-can.

Film can
by Dr. J.J.

I whipsawed between determination and despair. Cursed myself and the heavens. Threatened to give up, then vowed I'd continue.

All in the same day. *Every day.*

Have you ever misplaced your sunglasses and turned the house upside down looking for them?

Was it frustrating? Even infuriating?

Exactly.

Now you're getting a tiny speck of the picture.

The difference is, I didn't simply search the house. I searched the whole wide world.

Literally.

And then one morning I was in Borneo, peering through binoculars at a chestnut-crested yuhina high in the branches of a Koompassia tree, when it suddenly dawned on me.

I hadn't looked for my CANN in more than a week. In fact, I hadn't even thought about my CANN in more than a week.

Hard to believe? Well, it's true. And the same thing would happen to you, I'm sure.

If you'd been ranting and raving and raging around the house for 15 or 20 minutes, searching for those sunglasses, sooner or later you'd pop your mouth wide open in surprise. Because out of the clear blue sky you'd realize you weren't turning over the cushions on the couch or patting the pockets of jackets in the hall closet.

No, not any more. You were stretched out in the Barcalounger, watching TV.

You wouldn't know how long you'd been there. You wouldn't even remember sitting down. But there you'd be, as relaxed as the last strand of spaghetti on a cold plate.

Still without your sunglasses.

I don't know how it happens. I just know it happened to me. And I'm pretty sure it would happen to you, too.

Notebooks
by Dr. J.J.

As I traveled the world looking for my CANN, I started paying more attention to the people and places around me and less attention to the search for my ride home.

And everywhere I went, I took notes. Lots of them. 15,151 pages worth, to be exact. Filled with facts, figures, questions, and even drawings about everything and everyone I'd seen and heard.

I have to be truthful, though. The stuff that you earthlings think is amazing – like the Suez Canal and the Hoover Dam and the Sydney Opera House – was a real yawn to me.

Other planets are much more advanced than yours, technology- and engineering-wise.

I'll give you an example: More than 6.5 million tourists a year visit San Francisco's Golden Gate Bridge. It's classified as one of the Seven Wonders of the Modern World, because it's the longest single-span suspension bridge on Earth.

It's 1.2 miles from beginning to end.

About 4,000 years ago – give or take a couple hundred years – the government of the planet Medred erected a bridge to the planet Yabble.

Which is 182,645 miles away.

And they did it just to do it. Because no one ever drives to Yabble. There's no place to park.

The truth about alien abductions

Aliens aren't interested in snatching earthlings for scientific study. Other life forms have been around for at least 12.36 million years, so they figured you guys out a long time ago. But they do enjoy watching your behavior. Lining up to sit on Santa's lap, chasing butterflies, reenacting the Civil War, putting your teeth under pillows, dressing dogs in human clothing, impersonating Elvis, wrestling alligators, and kicking, hitting and chasing balls all over the place . . . you're an alien's version of un-reality TV. Now that I live here, my favorite earthling pastime to watch is bungee jumping, especially at the 720-foot Verzasca Dam tower in Ticino, Switzerland. It was featured in the James Bond film *GoldenEye*. Every time I see someone plunge from the precipice with nothing to stop the free fall but a stretchy latex cord, one word comes to mind: iirknl, which, loosely translated, means CRAZY.

I don't mean to come across as critical. But when I saw the so-called "marvels" of Earth, I had the same reaction a mathematics professor might have when he learned that his four-year-old son could count to 100:

Good job. Now keep going.

I did find lots of other things about life on Earth amazing, though. In time you'll hear about them all.

Right now I want to tell you about trying to get home, then realizing I already am.

And about what I've learned about being a human being since I've been here.

Paladinos are *not* human. As I said, we're zibizzibiz. I can't really explain exactly what that means and, besides, it isn't the point.

The point is that Paladinos are different from earthlings in many of the same ways earthlings are different from squirrels or goldfish or mountain goats. And I'm not talking about looks.

I'm talking about the fact that we Paladinos spend most of our lives existing, not *living*.

We don't have to worry about paying our bills. Thanks to our superior intelligence and the exceptional educational system on our planet, Paladinos have numerous career options and command astronomical salaries, no pun intended. Lucky for us, because if you think a trip to Europe is expensive, try traveling to another universe.

We don't have to worry about having a roof over our heads. The Minister of Relocation, Permanent Accommodations and Tenancy – we call the minister MR PAT – relocates all Paladinos who are too old to continue living in Underage Paladino Shelters (UPS). Once our living quarters have been assigned, we're classified as "down PAT" and never move again.

We don't have to worry about safety. Because Paladinos only get upset at situations, not at other Paladinos, physical violence doesn't concern us. We might smash a defective remote activator button against a wall, but we'd never smash our fist in another Paladino's face.

All in all, I'd be willing to speculate that Paladinos are the most successful, settled and secure creatures in the cosmos. But since I've been on Earth, I've come to believe that even a poor, homeless, frightened earthling has a richer existence than a prosperous, protected Paladino.

Earthlings have feelings and friends and freedom. Paladinos only have reactions and associates and assignments.

On Paladin, everything is based on science and technology. Government officials program our entire lives using complex computer algorithms designed, at least in theory, to maximize the efficient acquisition and allocation of zibizzibiz resources.

There's no room for chance. Or choice.

For love. Or even like.

For passion. Or a sense of purpose.

You humans don't realize just how lucky you are. But I do.

That's just one of the things I learned during the last six years from the very first friend I ever had in my life, and from people I met at work.

You heard me correctly: *at work*. I haven't been bumming around all these years, mooching off others or relying on government welfare. I've been a productive, pay-my-own-way member of society.

I didn't pay for my lessons, though. I picked those up just by interacting with earthlings.

There are 10 of them, and more than a few have to do with loving freely. But love isn't all you need, no disrespect to the Beatles. Thinking and living by design also play big roles.

See for yourself:

Lessons for being human

1-Love someone
2-Love something you do
3-Appreciate your parents
4-Be kind
5-Keep growing
6-Use your brain
7-Believe in something bigger than yourself
8-Exercise your free will
9-Take care of your health
10-Eat sardines!

I'll explain more about the lessons soon. But first, let me introduce you to my best friend and most influential teacher.

And don't forget: This isn't a science fiction fairy tale.

It's a first-person account about being a human, not an alien, on Earth.

A beautiful planet
by Dr. J.J.

Chapter 3
Getting Duped

The rain stopped just as quickly as it had started. By the time I reached Mulberry Street on that wet day so long ago, femans were beginning to spill out of storefronts and restaurants. The ones who'd been caught without umbrellas were as soggy as I was.

That was good. Very good, in fact.

If I wanted to leave here in a travel CANN, not a police car, I couldn't attract attention to myself.

I tried to appear casual and comfortable as I looked around for someone to help me. There were a dozen earthlings on my side of Mulberry and 10 more on the other.   Tall, short, fat, thin, old, young – femans of every type were just a few steps away. Which one should I ask?

An old, short, fat one? A young, tall, thin one? Maybe a young, short, fat one?

How about the Blump wearing pink shoes, purple pants and a pink shirt? Paladinos are extremely color-sensitive, so I found the creature's clothing almost intoxicating.

Then I reminded myself that it was Blumps who got me into this mess in the first place. Asking one of them for help would be asking for trouble.

That cut my choices down to five.

Just pick one, I told myself. Any one. It doesn't matter.

I threw my shoulders back once more. Maybe the movement would send a "start walking" message to my legs.

But still I stood there, playing with the remote activator button in the right pocket of my pants. I turned it over and over again between my thumb and index finger, hardly aware of what I was doing.   I wasn't worried about accidentally pressing the button. Nothing could or would happen unless I was within three feet of my CANN.

Something made me repeat those last few words: . . . *unless I was within three feet of my CANN.*

Yes, yes, YES!! Why hadn't I thought of it before?

I didn't need help from an earthling. I could handle this on my own. All I needed was a little time.

Time to walk up and down Mulberry Street and the surrounding blocks. I'd push the button and say "Paladin" every few steps. Sooner or later I was bound to come within three feet of my CANN.

It had to be close by. I'd been gone from the lot for less than two hours. Barely long enough for the clean-up crew to bag the trash and toss it in a Dumpster.

I didn't need to *find* my CANN. I didn't even need to see it or touch it. I just had to come *near* it and say "Paladin."

Then I'd be instantly vaporized and transported home. And if someone saw me disappear into a blue brake fluid container and take off into the sky, what did I care?

I was never coming back to Earth again.

And I do mean *never*.

I started up the street, confident that I'd soon be smoking and drinking on my balcony.

Push.   Paladin.

Push.   Paladin.

Push.   Paladin.

Push. Paladin.

Push. Paladin.

Push.Paladin.

I walked and walked and walked, being careful to bump up against every box, bag, litter basket, trash barrel and Dumpster along my route.

Bump. Push. Paladin.

Garbage can
by Dr. J.J.

Nothing that was halfway big enough to hold a travel CANN escaped my eye. Or my thigh.

I was moving toward a packing crate in the alley to my left when I suddenly tripped. Over a someone, not a something.

A someone lying on the pavement.

"Hey, man, why don'tcha watch where you're going? Just who do you think you are anyhow, stepping all over a fellow trying to catch a little catnap? You could've broken my leg. You could've broken my neck. What in the world's the matter with you? You think you own this alley or something? And what're you doing in here anyhow? Don't you know guys get killed in alleys every day? Careless guys, just like you."

The tongue-lashing came from a feman who was now upright eight inches in front of me. About my height. Wearing a blue shirt with "U.S.A." in red letters. Black boots. Dark curly hair under a white cap. Brown eyes.

And head cocked. Like someone expecting answers.

But I couldn't even think about the questions, let alone what my answers should be. I was too busy concentrating on the first words the feman had said to me:

"Hey, man . . . ."

On Earth, I was a man.

It was news to me.

Back on Paladin, I'd never taken "The United States: Its People and Cultures" class. Every destination in the universe had its own seminar, but only travelers who planned to spend time in their DTTs were required to attend them.

Like I said before, I never spent time here. Or anywhere else, for that matter.

I only spent money. Other Paladinos came home from their trips with suntans and souvenirs. I came home with grocery bags.

Everything I needed to know about other people and cultures was contained in LASCO 76.9.14:

Residents of other planets had a tendency to turn aliens into cadavers and carcasses and then to disassemble, dissect or otherwise destroy them for the purpose of scientific investigation and/or possible replication.

Now that was information worth having. So were the addresses, marked on each of my DTT maps, of the best places to shop. All the other stuff would be as useful to me as a blow-dryer to a bald man.

Just now, though, without asking for it, I'd been given a piece of people-related information.

The fact that I was a man meant earthlings who looked like me were males.

And the curvy Blumps were females.

Interesting. In a completely useless sort of way, of course. It wouldn't help me back on Paladin.

Which was where I'd be very soon.

I turned my attention back to the feman . . . back to the man, that is . . . standing right in front of me. I had to say something to keep him from asking more questions.

There are 6,912 different languages spoken on Earth and I know 374 of them. Plus another 1,859 from other planets. Learning a foreign tongue is as easy for a Paladino as quacking is for a duck.

Knowing them isn't the same as being able to speak them fluently, however. That takes practice.

But if I concentrated hard, coming up with a brief explanation and apology for the curly haired man would be challenging, but not impossible. After all, I always spoke a little English on my shopping trips. It helped me avoid attracting attention to myself.

You see, I'd had an opportunity on my first visit to Newark to make a valuable observation: Nothing gets a store

> **The truth about alien invasions**
>
> Aliens don't need land, food, or water from other planets. Scientists control birth and death rates, so overpopulation can't occur. They never run out of things to eat or drink, because 80 percent of nutrition is chemically created. (Gabba 16-12 amylase is the most popular food on Paladin. It comes in a fat tube and tastes like a gooey mixture of almonds, paste and honey.) They don't have a desire for power or a need to conquer, because those are strictly human drives. Aliens visit other planets to sightsee, shop or people-watch. Period. They're tourists, not warriors. Earth is more likely to be attacked by hungry polar bears than by invading aliens.

clerk more riled up than a rude customer. The ones who don't speak or make eye contact, no matter how much the clerk tries to engage them in casual conversation.

So riled up, in fact, that I could still hear the employee's angry complaints about me from the sidewalk outside Bifano's.

My experience at the store had worried me quite a bit. For an alien, even the "Hello, how are you, would you like to have coffee someday?" kind of attention could be bad.

The yelling, cursing, stomping and pointing kind of attention was worse.

And the only kind of attention worse than the worse kind is the worst of all:

Spending infinity as a specimen. In a clear jar. On the windowsill of a junior high school biology classroom.

Swimming in your own juices, plus a couple of smelly chemicals designed to keep you looking clean and fresh.

Being stared at by class after class of students who don't understand – or don't care – that they're looking at slices of what was once a living creature.

Nobody wants that much attention. Not even a movie star.

I know what you're probably thinking. That I sound melodramatic and paranoid every time I describe the consequences of being identified as an alien.

But you read LASCO 76.9.14, didn't you? If you think the lawmakers were making up all that dissection stuff, you're wrong.

Paladinos always tell the truth. Even Paladino politicians.

Besides, until you've walked around all by your lonesome on Neptune or one of the other planets in the Milky Way, don't even bother talking to me about phobias.

The attention I'd attracted at Bifano's was a serious matter and I gave it serious thought. Which led to a pretty simple conclusion:

Failing to interact with a store employee was obviously considered as rude by earthlings as showing up in a government office with your gills uncombed was by Paladinos.

Once I understood the problem, the solution was easy. I took out what you might call a little death and dismemberment insurance.

I started speaking to store clerks.

A polite "hello" was first.

What came next depended on where I was.

At Henry's I'd point my finger at the desserts and say "cheesecake, please." At Bifano's, I'd point my finger at the items behind the counter and say, "Twelve bottles of Pappy's and five boxes of Madrons, please."

"Thank you" was last. I'd be sure to look the clerk in the eye and say it with a smile.

Then I'd pick up my shopping bags, scoop my change off the counter, and leave.

It had worked every time. No more bad attention. Hardly any attention at all, in fact.

If I could make eye contact and speak with store clerks, I could do the same with the irritated man standing in front of me, still with his head cocked.

I was as frightened as a field mouse in a room full of elephants. But I met his steady gaze, twisted my face into what I hoped was a happy expression, and opened my mouth to answer his question.

"Bjzy," was all that came out.

I pursed my lips together in concentration and tried again. "Bjzy swlin kpzg erlx rnlud mpzoi."

Before I could make a third attempt, the man stomped his boot on the asphalt.

"What in Sam Hill and blue blazes is wrong with you, mister? You crazy in the head or something? I can't understand a single word you're saying. If those noises can even be called words. You know what you need to do? You need to quit bothering me. Go on and get out of here quick as you can. And I mean it. Take your gibberish-talking self and move along.

"And don't wake me up again," he ordered.

But he didn't really seem to be angry or upset. He just seemed sleepy.

That was good. My walk-bump-push-and-say system was too time-consuming. I needed to go back to my original plan.

If I asked the earthling to tell me who had cleaned up the lot, he'd be too sleepy to ask a bunch of questions. He'd just give me a name and address and go back to his nap.

I took a deep breath, wiggled my toes to get my gills moving, and asked, "Have you any information regarding the identity of the local inhabitants who cleared the diminutive vacant lot proximal to Mulberry Street of all detritus?"

I knew I had violated KISSeR And forgotten my New Jersey accent. But I thought I'd done pretty well under the circumstances.

The earthling clearly didn't agree.

"Huh?"

He inched closer to me.

"I said huh? What did you just say to me?"

Then he quickly held up his hand and shook it from side to side.

"Never mind. You can forget about *what* you said. I can figure out that gobbledygook for myself. What I need you to explain is the 'why.' *Why* did you just say that to me?"

I muttered something that didn't make sense, even to me. But it didn't matter. The man wasn't listening.

"Nobody in his right mind talks that way. You know why? Cause nobody in his right mind would understand him if he did, that's why. Where're you from, anyhow? Mars?"

Gulp.

Gulp again.

What had given me away?

Sure, "bjzy swlin kpzg erlx rnlud mpzoi" sounds strange to earthlings. But six weird words do not an alien make.

I had hardly finished the thought when he started talking again.

"One thing's for certain, mister. You're not from around here," the man continued. "Cause I'd have seen you before if you were. I've been on these streets plenty long enough to recognize who's a stranger and who isn't."

He slowly walked around me in a circle, moving his eyes up, down and across as he went. None of the Martians I knew had tails, but this man seemed determined to find one on me.

When he was finally satisfied that I had everything I was supposed to have and nothing I wasn't, he stood in front of me again. And poked my chest with his index finger.

"Now that I think about it, you babbled just like one of those fancy-tongued graduates from one those highfalutin private schools. One of those places in Switzerland or Massachusetts that teach rich folks how to speak but not how to talk."

I just stared at him. Silently.

Words were popping through my head as fast as bubbles rushing to the surface of boiling water. Words like "beseech." "Entreat." "Implore." "Importune."

But I had a feeling that saying them out loud would only make matters worse. So I told myself to stay quiet.

The man took my silence as confirmation.

"That's it, isn't it? I'm right on the money. No pun intended. Mama and Papa Millionaire sent you off to boarding school so they could fly around the world and play with their rich friends. They didn't have time to take their little boy to DisneyWorld or help him with homework. No time. No interest.

"I know I'm right. I can see it all over your face. I can see that the way your parents treated you still bothers you to this day. Just like a bur inside your shirt collar.

"Well, let me tell you something, mister. Those people did you a favor. A BIG favor, in fact. That's my opinion, anyhow. And believe me, I know what I'm talking about. But it's something you're just going to have to figure out for yourself someday. You can't take my word for it."

If he had read hurt in my expression, my attempt at looking calm and detached had clearly failed.

And his facial detective work still wasn't over.

"I can see surprise in your eyes, too. Surprise that I figured it all out," he said. "Well, I can't take a lot of credit for that one. It was as easy as getting a ball to roll downhill.

"Truth is, every word that came out of your mouth a minute ago was straight out of an ad for a frou-frou prep school. Your frou-frou school and all the others just like it. Buy a New York Times on Sunday and you'll see exactly what I mean."

He moved back a foot or so and waited for me to react.

"Well, why don't you say something? Something like 'you're right' for starters."

I was scanning my brain as fast as I could, trying to locate words from what the travel camp coaches called the common vernacular.

But at the moment I couldn't even remember what the term meant. Find examples? I might just as well have searched for a snake with feathers.

Once again, however, I was saved by the earthling's tendency to fill in his own blanks.

"You just don't want to talk about your past, do you? Still makes you mad and hurts your feelings?" he asked.

The best reply so far had been no reply. Why change my strategy now?

"OK. That's your business, mister. And I respect it. Just so you know, I understand where you're coming from a lot more than you might think. A whole lot more, as a matter of fact.

"But that's another story. For another time."

He said the last two sentences in a way that seemed to offer proof of his understanding, rather than a promise of information to come.

I couldn't be sure, of course. This was my first extended interaction with an earthling.

First and last.

Even better: first, last and *over very soon.*

If he'd only stop talking long enough for me to squeeze in a question: Do you know where the trash removed from the vacant lot near Mulberry Street was taken? If not, do you know where I could find someone who does?

Straight out of the common vernacular.

Surprised?

Don't be. I'd had the earthling's help.

He'd been doing all the talking, not me. I'd just been standing there, acting like I was listening. Fact is, my brain was working hard and my ears were hardly working.

I'd had all the time I needed to find the right words, form sentences, and even practice them in my head. But I wasn't going to get a chance to say them out loud yet.

"I'll tell you one thing, though. I like a fellow who keeps private things private. Most people'll flap their gums about anything to anybody. Don't know the meaning of discretion. Love the sound of their own voices. Never met a story they couldn't top," the earthling said with a shake of his head.

"Glad to meet someone who isn't like that. Even if he sounds like some kind of crazy foreigner when he does talk."

With that, he stuck his hand out toward me and said, "Name's Dupe. What's yours?"

If a news anchor had just announced that Pappy Van Winkle's 90.4% Proof, 20-Year-Old Wheat Recipe Family Reserve Kentucky Bourbon was actually distilled from rice in a factory in China, I couldn't have been any more dumbstruck than I was at that very moment.

My Paladino name was Symzwnqhkkc Lieoijzjtrrr.

And it didn't translate into English.

Worse yet, I couldn't recall a single earthling-type name. Because there weren't any stored in my memory. And never had been.

Remember? In-and-out travelers like me weren't required to take the people and culture seminar.

We learned thousands of words at travel camp. And zero names.

So what do you think I said?

Exactly.

Nothing.

Dupe withdrew his hand and stepped back. He stood and stared at me, still as a photograph.

I did my best impersonation of a placid Paladino. If the man could see how nervous I was about being asked my name, he might go right back to his Martian theory.

I was silent on the outside, but on the inside I was torturing myself with thoughts of the horrible fate that awaited me because I had no name. Just as I'd reached the part where I'm taken to a laboratory for carving and cutting, Dupe began talking again.

"OK, I get it. I sure do. And I should've thought of it before. Your family isn't just rich. It's famous, too. If you tell me your name, I'll know everything about you. All the stuff you're trying to hide from me and everyone else.

"I get it, mister. I get it to the bone. You're running away from your future. Same as I did myself. But don't worry. It's cool. Your secret's safe with me."

Then he slapped me on my back and said, "Pick a new name for yourself when you're ready. As far as I'm concerned, that's who you'll be. In the meantime, I'll just call you 'Buddy'."

Dupe's assumption that I was running away from a rich and famous future had somehow turned his irritation into sympathy. Frankly, I didn't care what he believed.

As long as it wasn't that I was a Martian.

Right about now you're probably thinking: You're not running away from a rich and famous future. You're just a stranded Paladino. And Paladinos don't lie.

You're correct on all counts. But if you think back on the conversation you'll realize that I didn't say anything untruthful.

Why, I hardly said anything at all.

Dupe bent over and tightened the shoestrings on his boots. Then he flashed a smile.

"Now, if I remember correctly, Buddy, you asked me a few minutes ago where the trash on the vacant lot near Mulberry Street had been taken. Well, I don't know myself. But I bet I can find you someone who does. Let's take a walk."

He had understood my question. He had also anticipated the second one I would have asked in the common vernacular if he had given me a chance.

And he was taking me to that someone. Without even asking why I wanted to find the trash.

Things were definitely looking up.

Chapter 4
Dupont Rockefeller Jackalone, Jr.

Dupe told me the vacant lot had probably been cleared by a "roving bunch of good Samaritans" from St. John's Roman Catholic Church.

"I guess they think they can earn time off for good behavior from Purgatory by sprucing up the blocks around the church. Because you never know when Jesus might decide to buy property in Newark," he said with a laugh.

Even though there are no direct translations in Paladino, I had learned the meaning of the English word "church" in vocabulary class, along with "heaven," "hell," "God," and "Satan."

We have no religion on my planet. The only higher power we recognize is the Office of Government-Originated and Operationalized Directives to Guarantee Our Destiny.

We call that office GOOD GOD. Quite coincidentally, of course.

But when Dupe talked about Samaritans, Purgatory, and Jesus, he might as well have been speaking Restaxanelo. It's the most difficult language in the universe to master, even for Paladinos, who are required to be at least centi-lingual.

I could figure out that Samaritans were good people, Purgatory was a temporary place of punishment, and Jesus lived somewhere outside the city. Beyond that, I didn't know.

And I certainly didn't care.

I was too busy praying, in a Paladino sort of way, that within the next 60 seconds, I'd be a sky-borne streak of blue on my way to a home-based happy hour.

Now *that* would be sheer heaven.

When we arrived at St. John's, the pastor, Father Patrick Moran, confirmed Dupe's theory. On the first Wednesday of every month, members of the Catholics for Clean Communities – the 3Cs, as the group was called – swept through the city armed with charitable intentions and boxes of industrial-sized trash bags.

Instantly, nervous excitement charged my entire body, causing my gills to flutter inside my socks.

Yikes.

Fluttering could lead to only one thing: Trouble, with a capital "T." Not because I was afraid Dupe or the pastor would look at my feet and see what was happening down there.

I was in trouble because I'm ticklish. VERY ticklish.

Each time the tips of my gills brushed up ever so lightly against my socks, I had to pinch myself to keep from giggling.

Giggling itself isn't bad. But giggling right out of the clear blue. In front of one man who just a few minutes ago was looking for your tail. And another who is a perfect stranger. And you need the help of both of them to get home.

Well, that doesn't sound like good behavior for anyone. Especially an anyone like me who could end up being sliced and stewed as a result.

So I'm sure you can understand why I was glad that a thigh can't scream. No matter how many times it gets pinched. Or how much pain it's in.

As I squeezed my skin to keep from giggling, Father Moran squeezed Dupe's shoulder and counseled him on the benefits of attending Mass regularly. When Dupe's only response was a smile and a shrug, the priest laughed and gave him a two-armed bear hug.

I had a feeling they'd had this discussion before.

Then Father Mo, as Dupe called him, told us what I'd been waiting to hear.

The bags of trash had been brought back to St. John's and thrown in the Dumpster outside.

My skin began to tingle again. There it was, just outside the priest's office window. A big, green can with my not-so-big blue CANN inside.

I'd walk over beside it, push my remote activator, and be out of there faster than you could say "presto change-o Paladino."

When I suddenly evaporated from the church grounds, Father Mo would call it a miracle. Dupe would immediately shift his figuring-out engine into high gear.

Whatever he decided were possible explanations for my vanishing act, I didn't think divine intervention would be high on the list.

If the police came, they'd find nothing but a bunch of garbage and two bug-eyed witnesses. Before long, the cops would go away, the witnesses would be declared cuckoo-nuts and the incident would be forgotten.

Nobody would blame the disappearance on extraterrestrials. So earthlings wouldn't start looking for aliens under every rock. Which would allow Paladinos whose DTTs included Earth to continue visiting without increased risk of detection.

And my little adventure would turn out to be a major blessing for believers in miracles and only a minor misfortune for me.

But then Father Mo said something that turned my tingles into twinges. The Dumpster's contents had been emptied into a city sanitation truck 20 minutes earlier and taken to the local landfill.

I silently cursed the Catholic cleaning crew and the truck driver. I hoped they'd all bypass Purgatory and head straight to the warm reception awaiting them at

The truth about UFOs

It's unlikely that you or anyone you know has seen a real UFO. Technological advancements have made it possible for Blazar-Ejected Trans-Astral Shippers (BETAs) to hover invisibly over other planets while watching events below. BETAs are the standard vehicle for multi-passenger exploration. The most common BETA carries up to 5,000 creatures and looks like a large, flat piece of sheet metal. Not like a flying saucer. The only flying saucers I've personally ever seen are in the Repository for Ancient Transit Systems on the planet Sootnard. They're big, heavy and slow, so only a collector would ever want one. Like that LeMay fellow in Tacoma who owned more cars than anyone else in the world, including Jay Leno. When he died, his family opened a 3,000-vehicle museum that even has a Flintstone-mobile. RATS would love to have one of those. Carriers from Earth are real crowd-pleasers because their design features have nothing to do with performance. Look at the fins on a 1959 Eldorado Cadillac. Understand what I'm saying?

Satan's underground barbecue.

Father Mo saw the effect his information had on my expression, but he never said a word about it. And he didn't ask what I was looking for in the trash.

I guess being a man of faith means you accept things as they are and don't ask a bunch of questions.

Dupe thanked him for his help. I nodded. And we both left.

As soon as we got to the sidewalk in front of the church, Dupe stopped, turned in my direction, and stood as still as a statue.

He looked me in the eye, cocked his head, and asked me what Father Mo hadn't.

What I'd lost. And why it was so important for me to find it.

I couldn't lie, even if I'd wanted to. But that was OK. The answers were easy. And I must have felt comfortable around Dupe, because replying in English was easy, too.

"My CANN. It has everything I need in it," I said.

I won't rehash the entire conversation that followed. Dupe said something about a needle in a haystack and suggested I buy another can at Bifano's.

I described the type, color and size of my CANN and explained that it was all I had brought with me from home.

Those last words were all Dupe needed to hear. He turned in the direction of the landfill and motioned for me to follow.

"Keeping something from your past is a good idea," he said. "Good for memories of what you left behind, if you want memories. Good for motivation to stay away, if you need motivation."

I'd known Dupe less an hour, but it had been long enough for me to realize he liked to figure things out for himself. In fact, the less I said, the more he figured.

And the more he figured, the more he drew the kinds of conclusions that would keep me from becoming an experiment or an exhibit.

You might call it a mutually beneficial communication process. We used it during our entire walk to the Essex County landfill. As Dupe talked about the importance of knowing what you want, and don't want, out of life, I kept silent pace beside him.

When we finally arrived at the landfill's entry gate, he told the watchman we needed to look through the piles of bags that had recently been dropped off.

Landfill gate
by Dr. J.J.

"All deliveries that come here, stay here. No exceptions," he said, waving us away.

For a second I found myself wondering why a person would be paid to guard garbage. Then the implications of what the man had said electrified those cells in my brain responsible for worrying.

It was only a matter of minutes before I'd be completely transformed from calm and confident to petrified and paralyzed. I had to snap out of it while I still could.

Once again, Dupe's talking came to my rescue.

"We're not here for a treasure hunt. All we want is one big, blue brake fluid can that was accidentally tossed in a Dumpster brought here this afternoon from St. John's Catholic Church. It has some things in it that my friend here needs and nobody else would want," he explained to the guard.

The man nearly exploded out of his uniform in agitation.

"Wait a minute. Wait just a stinking doggone minute. Did you say brake fluid? Don't you know it's against the law to dispose of hazardous waste anywhere except at a designated recycling center? We don't allow that kind of stuff here. None of it.

"And lemme tell you both something right now. If we find that can, and if it contains even one drop of dried brake fluid, St. John's will have to pass the collection plate twice next Sunday. Once for the poor and once for the fine," he said.

Dupe didn't wait to hear the end of the warning. He turned back toward town and motioned for me to follow.

"I should've thought of that," he said with a snap of his fingers. "I'm as sure that the 3Cs hauled your brake can to the recycling center as I am that watermelons don't have tear ducts. Why, they'd think it was a mortal sin not to.

"It's getting so you can't even throw away your money without some government agency telling you how and where to do it. But this time, Big Brother messed up. The rules make less trouble for us, not more. Finding your can back at that dump would have been harder than tying Christmas bows with your teeth. But at the recycling center, all the stuff that somebody decided is toxic and causes six-legged cats is nice and organized.

"I've seen it myself. Paint cans are with paint cans, oil pans are with oil pans, and so it goes, right down the list of every single substance that helps us when we need it and supposedly kills us once we don't. If picking out your big blue container from all the other junk in the warehouse isn't as easy as spotting a blonde in Baghdad, then we both need guide dogs and white canes.

"You'd just better get prepared for what you'll see when you look inside the can. For what you won't see, I mean. Between the rummage hunters and the public servants, I'm 100 percent sure that something you took with you from home will be missing. And 99 percent sure everything will be.

"And don't bother thinking your things are safe because they only have sentimental value. You're wrong. A natural-born scavenger would just as soon holler 'finders' keepers' over a pair of bronzed baby shoes as over a pair of solid gold earrings."

Dupe had done it again. He had filled my brake fluid container with keepsakes from the home he imagined I had left behind. Just as he had earlier filled the silence after his questions with answers he imagined I was trying to keep secret.

You and I both know that when we found my CANN, it would contain exactly what it had when I left Paladin.

Nothing.

Except, of course, a mysterious technology. Which couldn't be stolen. Because it couldn't even be seen.

You and I also know that Dupe would never find out that my CANN was empty. As soon as I got close enough to it, I'd push the handy-dandy remote accelerator in my pocket and whisper the magic word.

Paladin.

Then it would be bye-bye Dupe. Bye-bye Earth. And bye-bye nightmare.

Estimated time of liftoff for my spaceflight was one half hour. That's how long Dupe had said it would take us to get to the recycling center.

In 30 short minutes I'd be canned vapor, heading home for my own private happy hour. The thought alone had the same relaxing effect on me as two fingers of Pappy Van Winkle's.

Well, not quite. But my nerves had definitely settled down after Dupe said it would be a cinch to spot my CANN at the warehouse.

My gills were still. My worry cells were inactive. Only my ears were in operation.

I was listening to Dupe explain how he'd figured out what I supposedly didn't want him to know. That I was running away from my rich-and-famous family and the rich-and-famous future they had planned for me.

He said he knew what I'd done because he had done the same. The only difference, he told me, was that while my rich parents had expectations for my future, his middle-class mother and father just had hopes.

Giuseppina and Antonio Giacalone were Italian immigrants who had come to the United States in 1980. Eight years after Marlon Brando won his second Best Actor Oscar for playing Vito Corleone in *The Godfather*.

Santa Maria! A man of Italian heritage had twice been awarded the top honor in his field. In their eyes, such a thing could only happen in a great country full of opportunity for people of all backgrounds.

Even those whose last names ended in vowels.

That very day, his parents had pledged that their children would be born and reared in the United States. They started working harder, saving more and spending less until they finally had enough money to make their dream of moving to America come true.

"I'm not going to bore you with the details, Buddy," Dupe said. "I'll give you just enough of the big picture so you'll see how we both ended up in the same place. Even though we started out in different universes."

Different universes. Was that another reference to my alien status?

I couldn't really tell. But he hadn't started circling me again, looking for a tail. So I decided I was out of danger for now.

Peanut and Tony, as they came to be called, immediately embraced their adopted country. They changed "Giacalone" to "Jackalone" out of respect for the English alphabet, which contains five letters absent from the Italian version, including "j" and "k."

When their son was born, they gave him first and middle names to match his Americanized last name. Not Michael or David or Paul. Those were the names of saints, not famous U.S. citizens.

Their child would be Dupont Rockefeller. The combination honored two captains of industry from America's past and captured the vision they had for their son's future success.

The man I knew as Dupe was actually Dupont Rockefeller Jackalone, Jr.

I wondered whether it was the kind of name I would have learned in the people and cultures class.

"There never was a senior," Dupe explained. "My parents thought junior made me sound like the son of a tycoon. 'The son of buffoons is more like it' is what my third-grade teacher used to say. She didn't like Italians much."

I guess the teacher's reaction answered my question. Dupe's name must be pretty unusual. Maybe that's why he ran away from Peanut and Tony.

"It never bothered me, though. Not the name or what people said about it," Dupe said. "Call me Joe Schmo or Jack Black, I'll still be exactly who I am.

"And as far as what other people think and say, well, I care as much about that as I care about whether penguins can add and subtract. It's just not relevant."

There went that theory.

Dupe's parents were fans of American capitalism, but not of American cuisine. They paid a cousin to send them boxes of meats, olives and cheeses from their hometown in Italy. What they didn't eat themselves, they sold from a wooden cart on a busy corner in Manhattan.

Eventually they were able to open a store that carried a full range of authentic imported Italian foods.

"My parents traveled more than 4,000 miles from Italy to settle in New York's Little Italy," he said. "They live above their shop, Mangiamo Bene! on Mulberry Street. Funny how I ended up on Mulberry Street, too, only across the Hudson in Newark."

Peanut and Tony reared Dupe on a diet of food from the old country and economics from the new. They read chapters from *Atlas Shrugged* and *The Fountainhead* to him at bedtime and hung Ayn Rand's photo on the dining room wall, next to Jesus, the Virgin Mary, and Antonin Scalia.

"I don't know what they taught you about Ayn Rand at that fancy-shmancy private school, but underneath all that bad writing is a whole lot of good thinking. Hemingway's easy to read, but hard to live by. He proved that when he killed himself. But Ayn Rand . . . she's just the opposite.

"Between my folks and me, we've got objectivism down to a science. Productive achievement courtesy Peanut and Tony. Self-interest courtesy me, myself and I.

"I do what makes me happy, Buddy. Simple as that. I don't take anything I haven't earned and I always pay for what I take, including the showers at St. John's or the soup at St. Vincent's. I don't own a car, a condo or even a cot. No sir. I like living on the street, even when the temperature's cold and the alley's deep with snow.

"Fact is, winter's when I realize just how lucky I am. I'm a man with nothing to lose. Most people think happiness comes from having more. Fatter paychecks and fancier homes. But the way I look at it, happiness comes from wanting less.

"If that's the case, then I have exactly what I want. And I plan to keep it that way."

He opened the door of the metal building ahead of us and motioned me through.

"Now, let's take a look around this recycling center and see if we can't find exactly what you want."

Chapter 4.5
You CANN't always get what you want

I stepped inside and immediately realized that what I wanted – what I absolutely had to have – wasn't there. In fact, nothing was.

The floor of the huge warehouse was as clean and clear as the vacant lot.

A clerk told us that on the first Wednesday of every month, recycled material at the local collection center is loaded onto a truck and taken to a district warehouse in Bordentown, nine miles away. Members of the 3Cs had arrived with their delivery, as always, just before the truck left.

Community-cleaning Catholics? Ha. As far as I was concerned the 3Cs stood for cursed altruism, confounded trespassing and contemptible punctuality.

The do-gooders were the Cause of Cataclysmic Consequences for me. I'd shortly be Caught, Cuffed and in Custody. Confronted, Cross-examined and Consigned to be Carved-up, in a Container of Chemicals.

Every panic-stricken thought that raced through my head ended in the same calamitous conclusion: It would soon be curtains for me.

My breathing was labored and I could feel my gills straining to take in air. I had to quit contemplating catastrophe and find a place to soak my feet.

Hose
by Dr. J.J.

On the grass outside the warehouse door, a man dressed in an orange jumpsuit was rinsing out a red plastic trash barrel he had turned on its side. I walked over, took the green vinyl hose from his hand and pointed it at my sandals.

Ahhhh.

As the cool water washed over my thirsty gills, I closed my eyes in relief. When I opened them, Dupe began laughing.

"I should've known you'd be a tenderfoot, Buddy," he said. "Rich guy like you probably grew up riding around in a chauffeured limousine. A 15-minute walk from St. John's and you're running for a pedicure.

"Just how do you plan to get to Bordentown? You going to call your parents and ask them to send their driver?"

The near hysteria I felt must have shown on my face, because Dupe quit making fun of me.

"Oh, we'll get there all right. Don't you worry about that," he said with a reassuring pat on my arm. "We'll go see Jimmy Malone. He'll take us first thing tomorrow."

Tomorrow seemed almost as far away as this morning did. I felt as if a lifetime had passed since I'd left Henry's Café.

I was afraid. I was exhausted. And, suddenly, I was very, very hungry. People on other planets lose sleep, weight or hair when they're stressed. Paladinos eat. And right now, I could consume an entire jrhkdibn. All by myself.

Dupe must have read my mind.

> ### The truth about microwaves
>
> Microwave ovens aren't alien secret weapons. They really are for heating and cooking food.* Excessive use of a microwave won't ever cause you to disappear spontaneously from your kitchen into outer space. I promise you – the only thing that will disappear as a result of excessive use of food preparation devices is your waistline.   (* Or for fun experiments. For example, put a light bulb, stem side down, in a glass of milk, heat it in the microwave and watch it glow.)

"The Malones live over on Jolly Street," he said. "Jimmy's Irish and as nice a fella as you could ever want to meet. His wife Domenica's Italian. She goes by Minnie, but there's nothing mini about her. As a matter of fact, I call her Mighty. As in Mighty Stubborn, Mighty Mad and Mighty Loud.

"Jimmy likes to stop off after work at the neighborhood bar for a couple of beers with his friends. But Mighty Minnie wants him home every night, drinking Chianti, listening to Frank Sinatra and eating pasta with her and her old mama, Rosa, who doesn't speak a word of English and, as far as I can tell, just sits around praying the rosary all day.

"Minnie's been trying to turn Jimmy into an Italian for 10 years. It hasn't worked so far, but I suspect she'll never give up.

"Mighty Minnie's also a mighty fine cook. And she loves anybody who loves to eat. So quit looking like you've just been sentenced to death and let's go have some dinner."

Sentenced to death?

How did he know? How *could* he know?

Fear and hunger were competing for my attention.

Pickling?

Pasta?

It was going to be a long night.

Chapter 4.6
But you CANN keep trying

A month later, I was still in Newark.

Jimmy drove us to the Bordentown facility and we got there before the truck. Because the truck never arrived.

It broke down on the Pulaski Skyway.

A crew came and offloaded the contents onto two smaller trucks. One went to a collection center in Hoboken; the other to Toms River.

When Dupe asked the supervisor at Bordentown where my can had been taken, he replied, "Your guess is as good as mine."

When he asked why the trucks hadn't hauled everything to Bordentown, the original destination, the supervisor replied, "Your guess is as good as mine."

Why didn't I die right there on the spot?

Your guess is as good as mine.

I can tell you that at the time, my head pounded, my heart palpitated and my gills shriveled up so tightly in fear I almost suffocated.

Dupe thought I was getting ready to faint and asked for a glass of water.

The supervisor handed him an unopened bottle. When Dupe passed it to me, I unscrewed the top. You can guess where I poured the contents.

The supervisor grabbed the bottle out of my hand and yelled that I was supposed to splash the water on my face, not my feet.

Dupe pulled me toward Jimmy's car.

"Stay calm, Buddy. Just 'cause we don't know where your can is right now is doesn't mean it's lost forever," he said. "It hasn't vaporized into thin air."

"We'll find it. We just won't find it today."

It hasn't vaporized into thin air?

My gills stood at attention. The hair on the back of my neck did, too.

Dupe's references to other universes, death sentences and vaporized cans were hitting awfully close to home. Home as in Paladin.

Could he really know about aliens arriving in CANNs, I asked myself? If he did, I could end up behind bars in *the* can. Or packed in juice in *a* can.

This isn't really happening, my brain screamed loudly in my head.

While I was contemplating my future – or lack of one – Dupe was moving on to other conversational subjects.

I couldn't be sure what he knew about me and what he didn't.

But I knew one thing for certain about him: He talked more than a milli-lingual translator at the Cross-Cosmos Communications Conference.

Chapter 4.7
It CANN take a long time

The next few weeks were full of stress and strain for me and my gills.

Jimmy Malone drove us to Hoboken to hunt for my CANN, but we were barred from entering the recycling center.

Of course.

The guard gave us the name of someone to contact . . . .

Who gave us the name of someone else to contact . . . .

Who gave us the name of the person in charge of all the people to contact.

Dupe made calls while we were at Angie Spanko's house, babysitting her and her husband John's three-year-old twin boys. Angie said the twins, who'd been born on Christmas Day when she was 45, were "a gift from God, but He forgot to include a battery charger for me."

On Thursday afternoons she put Dupe in charge while she went out for what she called a "save Mommy's sanity" break. While the boys napped, Dupe called everyone on the list.

After finally reaching someone, somewhere, who knew something, he hung up the phone and said, "The good news is that we can look for your can at Hoboken and Toms River. The bad news is we have to wait until the second Thursday of next month."

I'll skip the part about the terror, torment and trembling caused by Dupe's announcement.

Let's just say that Dupe couldn't understand why I spent a full half-hour in the bathroom, and Angie couldn't understand why she found a stack of neatly folded wet towels in the tub when she came home.

My gills understood, though.

Chapter 5
On the job with Dr. J.J.

Once I accepted the fact that I was going nowhere fast, I realized I had to find a place to live.

I'd spent the nights since my arrival sleeping in alleys, under bushes, on porches, or in the back seats of cars at the junkyard with Dupe, and I couldn't do it anymore.

Dupe meant it when he said it didn't bother him, though. He slept wherever he happened to be when the sandman paid him a visit.

Just the other day, the two of us were walking through an alley, talking about whether poker is a game of strategy or chance. After finishing a story about a man in Singapore who won a million-dollar pot with only a pair of sevens, Dupe's eyelids started to flutter and his legs got a little wobbly.

Those are sure signs that he needs a quick nap. Right away.

He half-stumbled over to a Dumpster, wedged himself between it and a brick wall, and pulled his cap over his eyes. In about 12½ seconds he had nodded off, dozing with his head on his forearm like it was a feather pillow.

Pillow
by Dr. J.J.

Me? I could no more get a good's night rest in an alley than I could sing opera in the Miss America pageant.

Not because I'm finicky or fussy. Because I'm afraid.

Do you know how hard it is to keep your eyes closed in a public space when you're worried about someone trying to steal your sandals and socks?

If that happened, it would be lights out forever for me. Formaldehyde is the ultimate sleeping pill, if you know what I mean.

Besides, I knew the days of soaking my gills in the shower at the St. John's parish center men's room were numbered. Sooner or later, one of those little old busybodies in the Altar Society was bound to investigate the wet footprints I left every day between the bathroom and the side exit door.

She'd think I was some kind of weirdo and report me to Father Mo. He couldn't allow weirdos in the Catholic Church, so he'd throw me out into the street.

At best.

At worst, he'd have me arrested.

So I'd end up in one of two situations: Soaking my gills in toilet water at the Newark Public Library. Or having my gills – and the rest of me – soaked in embalming fluid.

No thank you to both.

I had to get an apartment. To get an apartment, I needed money. And to get money, I needed a job.

The cash I earned helping Dupe work construction wasn't enough to cover rent. Besides, the project would be finished soon.

Dupe would find other odd jobs to keep him in cannoli. He could do everything under the sun, to use an earthling expression. Plumbing, electrical work, carpentry, masonry, cabinetmaking, appliance repair, auto maintenance and anything else you can think of.

He got paid not only in money, but also in home-cooked meals, clothing, transportation and "you need it, you've got it" friendship.

But I had to have steady employment – of the fulltime, minimum-wage-or-more variety.

On Paladin I was an actuary responsible for designing and pricing retrocession schemes to maintain equity market stability. It was theoretical make-work, however, because the only investor on the planet is the government. I wouldn't have a clue how to deal with the complexities of real financial systems.

So I bought a *Star-Ledger* and leafed through to the classifieds. Reading the newspaper had gotten me into this nightmare to begin with. Maybe it could help get me out of it.

Short-order cook. Administrative assistant. Bulldozer operator. Tailor's helper.

I couldn't cook, take dictation, run heavy equipment or sew.

I did know how to eat, drink, smoke and travel. But I didn't think anyone would pay me to do it.

What, on Earth, could I do?

I was running through a very short list of possibilities in my head when I saw an ad inside a thick black border.

REPORTER WANTED

The *Newark Star-Ledger* seeks an individual with writing, organization, and people skills for position as weekly columnist. Qualified candidates will be enthusiastic, flexible, willing to travel and capable of easily learning new tasks. Previous reporting or writing experience necessary.

Send resume and supporting documents to:
HR Dept., 1 STAR-LEDGER PLAZA
NEWARK, NEW JERSEY 07102
The *Newark Star-Ledger* is an Equal Opportunity Employer

Interesting.

I could write. In fact, my high school PAL composition teacher once called me "gifted."

I was organized. Most frequent travelers are. Think about what you had to do to get ready for your last vacation. Now multiply that by more than a hundred trips and a gazillion miles.

My reputation as a go-along, get-along Paladino took care of the people skills issue.

I desperately needed a job, and the thought of finding one made me very enthusiastic indeed.

Was I flexible? Besides finding my CANN, I had no responsibilities or obligations.

As for my willingness to travel . . . well, I think the answer to that one is obvious.

So far so good.

Regarding the part about easily learning new tasks, I'm a quick study. All Paladinos are. Our brains contain a huge number of mirror neurons, which make us perfect mimics.

That's a whole 'nother story, but for right now I'll just say this: We can watch someone do something, then turn right around and do the same exact thing, the same exact way, ourselves.

It doesn't work with thinking, though. I could stare all day long at an engineer with a design in his head of a perfect perpetual motion machine and still not be able to build it myself.

But it seemed unlikely that a newspaper reporter would be asked whether a compact Riemann surface M of genus at least two could be embedded into a quotient of $SL_2(\mathbf{C})$ by a discrete cocompact subgroup.

So I checked off the easy learner requirement.

The final qualification was reporting or writing experience. Who in the universe doesn't have that?

Not only had I produced my fair share of letters, reports and homework assignments, I'd also composed a million stories in my head about the people and places I'd seen on my travels. If I could think it, surely I could write it. Even though my mirror neurons would be of no benefit.

A single obstacle now stood between me and full employment.

I needed an earthling identity. Which meant I needed Dupe's help.

Quick, fast, and in a hurry.

I found him on the construction site, measuring a string he'd wrapped around a drainpipe, then calculating something on a napkin.

"I'm stretching my figuring-out muscles a little bit," he told me when I asked what he was doing. "If I divide the string's length by pi, I'll know the diameter of the pipe and can tell the crew how deep to dig the trench to the street.

"It's about as hard as getting Donald Trump to talk about himself, but even the easiest kind of thinking is better than no thinking at all."

I was about to give him a challenge that would stretch his figuring-out muscles from one side of New Jersey to the other.

Or so I thought.

"Wooooo-weeeeee!" he shouted, clicking his heels together after he heard about my predicament. "Wooooo-weeeeee! You have no idea what you've just done for me, Buddy. No idea at all. In less than a minute you solved a problem I've been trying to figure out for 12 long years. You surely did, and I can't thank you enough. Now, just let me sit here and grin for a minute or two and then I'll tell you what we're going to do."

His reaction reminded me of the day he presented Mrs. McVitty, an elderly volunteer at St. John's, with an eight-week-old puppy we'd picked up at Jimmy Malone's on the way to the church. When Mrs. Mac squealed with delight at the tiny ball of fur's wet kisses, Father Mo winked at Dupe, who responded by sitting silently in a chair for a few moments, head bowed, smiling from ear to ear.

He later explained that Mrs. Mac arrived at St. John's every day before sunrise and stayed till after dark, polishing the wooden pews, burnishing the brass chalices, and ironing the altar linens. Fearing that the long hours would take a toll on her health, Father Mo had repeatedly asked her to stay home and let staff members handle the tasks. But Mrs. Mac wouldn't listen.

Dupe knew the puppy would do what Father Mo couldn't.

"Now she has to spend more time at her own house and less at God's," he said. "The puppy needs her. And she needs the puppy."

I hoped Dupe's epiphany regarding my dilemma wouldn't involve a small animal. My ticklish gills couldn't take being probed by a cold nose and a slobbery pink tongue.

"Here's the situation," Dupe said, rising from his reverie and bringing me out of my own.

"Number one: You can't tell the newspaper your real name and Social Security number because detectives hired by your rich family will track you down and force you to go home.

"Number Two: I never use my real name and I've never used my Social Security number.

"That leads us to Number Three, which is: You're welcome to them both."

He reached into his back pocket and retrieved a small envelope made of two Catholic prayer cards taped together on three sides. Then he put his fingers inside and pulled out a paper rectangle.

"There it is, Buddy. Nine numbers on a piece of paper worth far more than its weight in gold to someone not born in this country."

I gulped. A minute ago Dupe had referred to my Social Security number. Now he was calling me an alien. Again.

And he expected me to pay him in gold to keep quiet.

I could almost smell the pickle juice.

"What this scrap of paper does for you and me and other Americans just like us is give us official status as card-carrying taxpayers of the United States. I don't make enough money to pay taxes, Buddy, and I sure don't want to be official," Dupe continued, unaware of my racing heart.

"So take my official card and my official name and go get yourself an official job. As far as I'm concerned, you're officially Dupont Rockefeller Jackalone, Jr. Which makes me just plain Dupe."

Social Security card
by Dr. J.J.

I waited for him to state his price, but all he did was shake the card at me impatiently. When I told him I couldn't take his name and identity, he told me not to worry.

"You're too twitchy and tense to be me, Buddy. You're always on edge. Scared looking, like you're expecting someone to jump out and yell 'Boo.' I thought rich folks knew how to look relaxed on the outside even when they were nervous on the inside. You definitely missed that lesson. Missed the whole semester is more like it.

"You have my name and number. That's the easy part. Mastering mellow is going to take some time. But don't worry, we'll work on it."

He slapped my back with his hat.

"Get it, Buddy? I told you not to worry about worrying. Most people notice little jokes like that. But you're as nervous as a beef cow at a barbecue, so I have to point them out to you."

He started walking back toward the stack of drainpipes when he suddenly turned toward me again.

"I know what's wrong. You can be Dupont Rockefeller Jackalone, Jr., but you can't be Dupe.

"I grew up in a neighborhood full of smart-aleck Italian kids. How do you think they said Jackalone? Try jack off, jack o' lantern, jack sh*t, jack rabbit or Jack Benny. Then one afternoon in high school I made a bad play at basketball practice and the coach said I was a stupid dupe. It caught on, and ever since I've been Dupe Fill-in-Your-Favorite. But I don't care about what

> ### The truth about time
>
> Repeatedly waking up in the middle of the night to find the minute and hour hands of your bedroom clock in alignment (e.g., at 1:05 or 2:10 or 3:15) or a digital readout of the same numbers (e.g., 3:33 or 4:44 or 5:55) is not a sign that you're an alien. It's a sign that you're probably an insomniac.

people call me any more than I care about whether a jelly bean can learn to walk. It's just not relevant.

"I'll keep Dupe. You take the rest. Call yourself Rocky, Feller, Jack or Junior. It's up to you. Now that you're Dupont Rockefeller Jackalone, Jr., there's finally a senior," he said with a shake of his head and a chuckle. "Me."

Dupe told me I needed to send a resume, so I sat under a tree and jotted down a chronology of my employment background on a napkin from McDonald's. Then I headed to the nearby FedEx Office.

I paid a teenage customer $30 to type my resume, a cover letter and three stories. One about cigars. One about bourbon. And one about vacation planning.

Two hours later, I stuffed the printed documents in an envelope and mailed it to the *Star-Ledger*.

With no return address.

Naturally.

I did include the number of the pay phone outside the local soup kitchen, where Dupe and I occasionally ate meals but more often served them. I said I could be contacted there between 1 p.m. and 2 p.m. any day of the week.

Not exactly a sign of flexibility, but what else could I do?

> **The truth about utility lines**
>
> Power lines interfere with flying, hovering and landing, so aliens steer clear of them. Literally. If you want to avoid aliens, move closer to power lines, not farther away.

Eight days after sending in my packet, Dupe and I were sitting on the curb outside the soup kitchen. We were hoping, just as we had every other day, that the next hour would bring an end to our waiting.

Three of the people in line for food had just started arguing about which were better, cake or yeast donuts, when the phone rang.

The newspaper wanted to interview me.

The HR person on the other end of the phone, a Mrs. Rosenblatt, said my resume was very unusual.

Of course. Translating experiences on Paladin into earthling-type jobs wasn't easy. It had required every single molecule in every single one of my "gifted writer" cells.

But their reaction to my stories had been very enthusiastic. According to Mrs. Rosenblatt, my writing "demonstrated an ability to conduct in-depth research on a variety of timely topics and write about them in a clear, concise, cogent and compelling manner that captures and keeps the reader's interest."

KISSeR had come through for me. Though Mrs. Rosenblatt could use a few lessons.

Dupe borrowed a suit for me from Jimmy Malone. He told me I looked like a fool wearing a double-breasted pinstripe with stretched-out white socks and sandals. I told him I had a superstitious nature and considered my footwear a good luck charm.

I talked to three people at the *Star-Ledger*: the editor, the managing editor, and the editor of the Living section, where the weekly column would run.

I won't bore you with all the details of what happened at the interview. I'll just give you the basics:

The editor, Mr. Frank Devereaux, told me that whoever was hired for the position would work at all kinds of jobs around the state and then write about them.

That was good news. Besides earning money, I could travel to places where my CANN might be.

Mr. Devereaux went on to say that unemployment in the Newark area was high and climbing. He thought stories about different occupations might help people find jobs or make career changes.

And, therefore, would boost circulation.

All of a sudden, before I even knew it was coming, an opinion flew right out of my mouth and landed with a splat in the middle of the room.

The best way to get more readers, I told the editor, was by covering news events on other planets.

I realized immediately what I had said and made a desperate attempt to laugh. "I was only joking, really I was," the pitiful, choking sound tried to say.

But Mr. Devereaux's lips were a thin white line between his nose and chin. He gave me an angry "you're either stupid or crazy" look and started to rise out of his chair.

Then he suddenly sat back down and slammed the palm of his hand down so hard on the top of his desk, I nearly jumped out of my own chair.

"You had me going there for a minute," Mr. Devereaux said. "By God and gumbo, you certainly did. I thought you were one of those druggie psychos who look normal on the outside . . . well, sort of normal anyhow . . . but are nothing but piles of twisted wire inside.

"You're absolutely right, though. Of course you are. New Jersey is the center of the *Star-Ledger*'s world. There's no doubt about that. But it sure isn't the center of the universe.

"By God and gumbo, we're going to open up this column to the rest of the planet."

With that he shook my hand, walked me to the door of his office, and said I should withdraw my application if I wasn't ready, willing and able to travel the globe.

He also advised me to buy a new suit. And some decent shoes while I was at it.

After taking a few tests to help the newspaper find out if I was some kind of nut and whether I'd follow the *Star-Ledger*'s rules, I left. Mrs. Rosenblatt told me on my way out that I would hear from her within three days.

I don't want to sound like an egotistical alien, but I felt pretty good about my prospects.

Mr. Devereaux had thought I was OK. The tests had been pretty straightforward. And I had worn my lucky landing outfit underneath the pinstripe suit.

I know what you're thinking: I was wearing those very same clothes when I lost my CANN.

And you're correct.

But faced with a "maybe they're lucky, maybe they're not" situation, I chose "they are." Paladinos are extremely optimistic creatures.

Once again, I was right. The very next day, Dupe and I had no sooner arrived at the soup kitchen when the phone started ringing.

I got the job!

Mrs. Rosenblatt said everyone at the newspaper thought I was a little quirky. But they decided maybe that was a good trait in someone whose job was to start and quit jobs on a regular basis, over and over again. Plus, as she had told me before, they liked my stories.

But what Mrs. Rosenblatt said had clinched the position for me was my answer to one particular test question.

She told me that my response showed "an advanced ability to consider the complex facts of a choice situation, evaluate the consequences and implications of alternative options, and produce a solution that is at once creative, optimal and operational."

I think she was trying to tell me that no one had ever thought of my answer before. But I wasn't sure. Mrs. Rosenblatt gave me a newfound appreciation for KISSeR.

A nanosecond later, the news sank in. In a few days I'd be a working alien.

Living in an apartment. Sleeping without fear of losing my socks and shoes. Soaking my gills in a bathtub. My *very own* bathtub.

I thanked Mrs. Rosenblatt. Then I asked her about the clincher.

Here it is:

You are driving down a familiar road during a dangerous, raging storm. Torrential rain, flashing lightning, booming thunder and falling tree limbs make you glad you're almost home. With less than a mile to go, you come alongside a bus stop, where three people are waiting:

    1. An old woman who looks as if she is about to die.

    2. A good friend who once saved your life.

    3. The perfect partner about whom you have always dreamed.

Which one would you offer a ride, knowing that your car has room for only one other person?

Before you start thinking about the question, you have to completely forget about a few things:

You and I both know that you can't possibly tell with just one glance that a stranger waiting for a bus is your perfect partner. I realize this even though Paladinos don't have partners, wives, husbands, girlfriends, boyfriends, or even friends.

Everyone in the cosmos understands that "perfect" exists in theory, but not in reality.

Also, squeezing an extra person or two in your trunk is probably not what the question-writer had in mind as an answer. It's just too obvious. Besides, you don't know anything about the size of the trunk or the size of the people.

And you can't think about the silliness of the situation itself. No one – at least no one you'd want riding in your car – would stand at a bus stop in the middle of such a powerful storm.

Number One, like the question said, it's dangerous.

And Number Two, everybody knows that no bus driver will go out on the road under those conditions. At least, not if the government or a union is involved.

But you just have to ignore the stuff on tests that doesn't make sense.

And don't bother asking for clarification or explanation. First, you'll mark yourself as indecisive. And second, one of two things will happen:

Your request will be refused flat out. Or the additional information will confuse you even more.

For example, suppose you asked why three people would even go to a bus stop on a wild and stormy night and then just stand there while Mother Nature was crashing all around them.

You'd probably be told something like this: "The people are blind, so they couldn't see the storm coming. And they continue standing at the bus stop because there's no shelter anywhere in sight, not even an awning or the eaves of a building. And even if there were shelter, which there isn't, the people wouldn't be able to see it. Because they're blind."

In my opinion, that kind of information would make things a whole lot more confusing, not less.

Because then I'd start thinking to myself, "OK, a bus stop in some place with no shelter anywhere around must be out in the middle of nowhere. Three blind people can't get to the middle of nowhere without help. So why don't the people who took them to the bus stop in the first place just come back and pick them up?"

My point is, try not to get distracted or start out-thinking yourself. Just answer the question.

Which of the three people would you have saved from the storm?

Here's what I wrote:

"I'd hand the car keys to my best friend and ask him to drive the old woman to the hospital. Then I'd wait for the bus with the partner of my dreams."

With those two KISSeR sentences, I gave the *Star-Ledger* the "best, happiest answer ever."

And the *Star-Ledger* gave me a job.

The next day I went to the newspaper office to fill out paperwork. A W-4, I-9, harassment policy, Internet-use policy, e-mail policy, vacation policy, retirement policy, non-discrimination statement, description of health and medical benefits, drug test release, copyright agreement – I signed and initialed every single one of them. Plus a few more I can't remember.

It probably sounds like a lot of red tape to you. But it was nothing compared to what's required to get a Pan-Universal Passport (PUP) back on Paladin. A background check. Medical exam. Physical ability test. Ethics and integrity analysis. Psychological assessment. Personality profile. Spatial orientation and directional referencing diagnosis.

Those and seven other screening procedures for a passport are the easy part. Filling out the stack of required forms is what's hard.

I knew a Paladino who finished the first 52 documents without a problem. Then he got up from his chair in the PUP office. He lifted the application computer over his head. And he hurled it through the glass door of the director's suite.

That Paladino traveled only once in his entire lifetime. Straight to prison.

So I didn't mind the paperwork at the *Star-Ledger*. Besides, I found out when I started at the newspaper a week later that the name for my new column came right out of all those forms.

On the Job with Dr. J.J.

You might not have thought about it before, but my initials are D.R.J., Jr. I wrote them dozens of times on the employment documents.

When Mrs. Rosenblatt's administrative assistant finished processing my paperwork, she sent Mr. Devereaux an e-mail and copied Mrs. Rosenblatt.

"The pre-hire review has been completed. Dr. J.J. is good to go," she wrote.

Mrs. Rosenblatt was upset by the assistant's "blatant lack of attention to detail." She demoted the young woman to the mailroom.

The editor loved it. He thought my real name was pretentious anyhow.

He added "On the Job" to the front end.

Mrs. Rosenblatt hired back the administrative assistant.

And everyone, especially me, was happy.

When I told Dupe about my newspaper name, it seemed to make him pretty happy, too.

"You're not a doctor of philosophy, psychology, chiropractic, osteopathy, medicine, education or legal letters. I guess that means you're a doctor of jobology," he said through snorts of laughter.

I didn't get the joke.

But that was OK. Dupe was enjoying it enough for both of us.

Chapter 6
A home away from home

I had a name, a Social Security number, a job and $3,500 the newspaper had given me to buy a MacBook computer, a digital camera, and an iPhone.

What I didn't have was a place to live.

"You don't need an apartment, son," Dupe said to me. "You want one. Confusing requirements and desirements is the root of most of the unhappiness in this world. I can see how years spent sitting on cushy chairs and sleeping with pillows would make you soft but, fact is, a quiet corner in an alley out of the wind and rain is more than enough for a man."

With that, he turned down the street and waved at me to follow him.

I didn't ask where we were going or why. It hadn't taken me long to learn that Dupe was always a few steps ahead of me – in his walking and his thinking – and that he always had a destination or a solution in mind.

Two blocks later, he knocked on the eggplant-colored door of a house and was greeted by a woman whose eyes were almost as black as her hair.

Front door
by Dr. J.J.

"Philomena Ventiglione, this is Dr. J.J.," Dupe said after the two of them finished hugging one another. "Dr. J.J., this is Phil."

Phil took her arms off Dupe's shoulders and put them around mine.

Since I'd begun traveling to Newark, I'd seen many earthlings hug. The first was on one of my earliest trips to Bifano's, when two enormous men at opposite ends of the bakery aisle spotted one another, let out what sounded to me like war whoops, and ran toward each other with their muscled arms outstretched in what I assumed were the wind-ups to a series of angry punches.

I dropped my Borsari Panettone Classico box and was halfway to the exit, gills on high alert, when I realized the two were laughing, not growling, as they embraced. Luckily, everyone else in the aisle was too busy smiling at the reunited friends to notice me retrieve my cake and slink back into line.

After that, I observed that greetings and farewells between humans were often accompanied by physical contact. Especially if one of the humans was Dupe. Everybody – men, women, boys and girls – wanted to hug him. And he seemed to enjoy hugging them right back.

Now it was my turn.

I'd never given or received a hug before. As I've mentioned, Paladinos have feelings, but they relate to situations, not people.

In my lifetime I'd felt afraid, aggravated, agitated, amused, annoyed, anxious, bored, calm, confident, confused, curious, disappointed, displeased, doubtful, energized, exhausted, fatigued, fearful, frustrated, grateful, guilty, impatient, irritated, optimistic, relaxed, reserved, restless, secure, sleepy, surprised, tense, uncomfortable, uneasy, and wary.

But I'd never felt love or like. Not for, or from, another Paladino.

There's no place for Paladino-to-Paladino emotion on my planet. The Paladino who threw an application computer through the glass door of the PUP director's office was frustrated at the situation, not at the person. He simply couldn't understand why a civilization as advanced as ours couldn't cut down on paperwork and red tape.

I had no practice hugging, or even touching. But how hard could it be?

I raised my arms and squeezed Phil. As I did, I felt the soft fullness of her lumps against my chest.

I pulled her closer.

"Whoa, son," Dupe cautioned me as Phil's sandaled feet rose six inches off the floor. "Don't get carried away just yet. Save the superhuman hug for after she has helped you."

Superhuman?

I know that Paladinos are among the strongest beings in the universe. And now that I've mentioned it to you, you know it, too. But there's no way Dupe could have known.

I glanced over at him to see if he was eyeing me suspiciously. I was close to moving in to an apartment and close to starting my job – both of which would put me closer to my home so far away. The last thing I needed was for Dupe to accuse me of being an alien invader. But he had already turned his attention from me and my hug to Phil and the explanation he was giving her about who I was and why we were there.

I should have known. I'd begun to feel safe from detection by Dupe. He reassured me every day that the parents he assumed were searching for me would never look in Newark because "to the super-rich, New Jersey is just a nicer name for a solid waste landfill."

The truth about mind reading

Wearing a hat made of aluminum foil won't keep aliens from reading your mind. Aliens won't read your mind because they can't. Besides, it isn't necessary. Earthlings will tell you anything you want to know if you simply ask. In fact, you don't even have to ask. Blogs, Tweets, chat rooms, away messages, status updates – they're on the Internet for literally everyone to read. So avoid an embarrassing fashion faux pas and save your foil for leftovers. If you want to cover your head, for men I suggest a hand-woven straw Panama hat by Borsalino in warm weather, or their felt fedora in cooler temperatures. I never leave home without one. For ladies, I recommend a stylish chapeau of modest size so as not to impede the view of others. Be prepared to be mocked by people who don't share your love of sartorial accessories. When Dupe informed me that men gave up toppers after John Kennedy's bareheaded presidential inauguration, I reminded him that his ball cap, by any name, is still a hat.

His reassurances were spoken with such conviction, he even convinced me. Not that my parents wouldn't search for me in Newark. No. He didn't have to convince me of that.

Paladinos don't have parents. We have progenitors. They donate the Paladino equivalent of DNA. TLC, if you can call it that, is provided by the Secretary of Infinite Species Survival and Sustainability. SISSY, as we refer to the secretary, runs the shelters where we live till we're old enough to work and serve in a SEX RoOM.

No one was looking for me in Newark because no one was looking for me at all.

Nevertheless, I looked forward to Dupe's reassurances because they were evidence he believed his own story about my being a runaway.

Phil appeared to believe it as well.

She's a former high school English teacher who now buys and renovates real estate. When Dupe told her I was a fugitive from my family, she handed me a set of keys and said I was welcome to rent the vacant side of her duplex as long as I didn't host loud parties, own the book *Poetic Gems* by William Topaz McGonagall, or hang dead animal trophies on the walls.

I agreed to each of her conditions, even though I had no idea what the latter two were about. I did, however, know about loud parties. And I had no intention of hosting one.

I'd recently accompanied Dupe to a St. Patrick's Day dinner at the Malones, where Jimmy and the other Irish chugged green beer, the Italians drank red wine, the rest of the guests sampled Extremely Exotic Sarahs and everyone – regardless of alcohol preference or ethnic persuasion – sang "Danny Boy" at the tops of their lungs.

All the while, Mighty Minnie's 70-year-old mother, Rosa, wearing a black dress and heavy black shoes, her hair in a silver knot atop her head, circled the room. She was sipping sherry from a crystal glass, giggling, and pinching unsuspecting men on their cheeks.

I was hanging out at the buffet table with my back to the crowd, keeping a low profile and popping profiteroles into my mouth, when the old lady tapped my arm.

As I turned, she reached her right hand to my face, twisted a piece of my skin hard between the knuckles of her index and middle fingers, and grinned, "Comme si bello."

Ouch.

If she really thought I was "so handsome," why did her compliment have to hurt?

Thankfully, when Dupe saw my look of pain and confusion, he whisked her away for an impromptu Tarantella.

There I was, a stranded alien desperately trying to avoid being pickled in a juice-filled bottle for eternity. Standing in a room full of pickled earthlings taking slugs from bottles so they could stay juiced all night.

Talk about needing a drink.

So when Phil asked me to promise not to have loud parties in her duplex, saying "yes" was as easy as singing the Paladino planetary anthem.

Sleeping in a comfortable bed. Soaking my gills in a tub full of cool, refreshing water. Imagining the excitement and relief I'd feel when I found my CANN.

That was my idea of a good time.

I couldn't wait for the fun to begin.

Chapter 7
A CANN do attitude

The second Thursday of the month finally arrived, and it fell on the day before I began my job at the *Star-Ledger*. Meaning that I'd be starting work on a Friday.

Mrs. Rosenblatt said it was newspaper policy.

"Research on the psychology of organizations has demonstrated a correlational, if not a causal, link between employee productivity and employee satisfaction," she said. "Day of the week has been found to be a reliable predictor of satisfaction in multiple regression models. More pointedly, the beta weight for Monday is negative and significant at a more conservative alpha level than those for other days. This finding is replicable even when using a Bonferroni approach.

"Here at the *Star-Ledger*, we believe that giving new hires the weekend off immediately after their first day results in higher productivity over their entire careers with us. Of course, we haven't tested that particular hypothesis. But, as I often tell Mr. Devereaux, if it makes sense logically, it makes dollars fiscally."

Huh?

I hadn't questioned Mrs. Rosenblatt about why the newspaper wanted me to start on Friday. I didn't care. The days of the week were all the same to me. But Mrs. Rosenblatt liked explaining things. Even if you didn't ask her to. Or didn't understand her explanation.

Her assistant was a pretty good translator, though. She said that because many workers dread Mondays and because the first day on a new job is always stressful, Mr. Devereaux decided the newspaper had nothing to lose by following Mrs. Rosenblatt's suggestion. Even if, he said, it was based on "nothing but cow manure and pure psychological, statistical and verbal mumbo-jumbo."

What the assistant told me was interesting. In a totally useless sort of way, of course.

Useless because, with a little luck and a lot of looking, today – the l o n g – awaited second Thursday of the month – would be the start of my trip home to Paladin and the end of my newspaper career before it ever started.

On the drive to the Hoboken landfill, Jimmy and Dupe sat up front, locked in a debate about who was the toughest guy ever to play pro football. I sat in the back having my own debate about whether sticking my head out the window would help stop the muscle spasms I

The truth about myths

A survey in the '90s of almost 6,000 Americans by a respected polling organization concluded that one out of every 50 people met the profile of an alien abductee. The markers were:

– Waking up paralyzed with a sense of a strange person or presence in the room. *Like the night Phil's 120-pound Irish wolfhound, Joyce, slept stretched across my bed at the Linger Longer Lodge in Montreat, NC?*

– Experiencing a period of time of an hour or more in which you were apparently lost but couldn't remember why or where you had been. *This happens to Mr. Devereaux every time he and Mama Rosa play Bloody Knuckles with a bottle of Campari and a deck of cards.*

– Seeing unusual lights in a room without knowing what was causing them, or where they originated. *Two words: Lava Lamp.*

– Finding puzzling scars on your body and neither you nor anyone else can remember how or where you got them. *Ask a tattooed sailor about this one.*

– Feeling that you were flying through the air, although you didn't know why or how. *Contrary to expectations, Mrs. Rosenblatt did not enjoy crowd surfing at last week's Music at Midnight concert.*

Aliens get the blame because fiction is more fun than fact. But the truth is, most bizarre occurrences stem from the strange behavior of ordinary humans.

was experiencing at the prospect of finally finding my CANN.

At the facility, the guard told us that hazardous waste "always goes to Toms River, and the bozo at Bordentown should have known that."

I wasn't familiar with the term "bozo," but based on the way the man spat the word, I guessed that he thought as little of the person at Bordentown as I did.

"We've bounced from landfill to landfill so many times, I'm starting to feel like a pinball in a Coney Island arcade," Dupe said.

"But that's OK. A trip to Toms River should give me just enough time to convince Jimmy that it took more guts for Jack Youngblood to play with a fractured leg than it did for Ronnie Lott to have part of a dislocated finger cut off. After Ronnie had his pinky shortened so he could stay on the 49ers' active roster, his pain was over. When Jack lined up for the Rams during the playoffs and the Super Bowl, his was just beginning.

"And if that doesn't make you change your mind, how about this little tiebreaker: Youngblood missed only one game in 14 seasons, and that was because he ruptured a disc. Doctors told him he needed surgery, but he wouldn't hear it. The man was back on the field the next week."

At this point, amputating an entire finger seemed like a small price to pay to get back home. But I'd be lying if I said lopping off a leg was an option.

No leg = no foot. No foot = no gills. No gills = no good.

Paladinos need a *pair* of gills in order to breathe better. It's based on the physiological principle of autologous reciprocal respiration, which I believe in without understanding one iota of how it works.

The same way earthlings believe in God.

By the time we reached Toms River, Dupe had persuaded Jimmy to his way of thinking.

"You can't keep holding a grudge about an exhibition game that happened in 1955," Dupe told him. "Sudden-death overtime was a good idea then and it's still a good idea. Every competition has to have a winner, Jimmy, and the Rams beat the Giants fair and square, 23-17.

"Besides, both teams agreed to the idea of a tiebreaker before the game even started. Now, I admit it's ironic that the Giants lost to the Colts in sudden death in the playoffs three years later, but you can't blame that on the Rams. And you sure as heck can't blame it on Jack Youngblood."

With that, he considered the matter settled and changed the subject to the benefits of artificial versus natural turf.

I had already noticed that Dupe cared nothing about always being right, but he cared everything about always being correct. When Phil chided him once for mispronouncing "flaccid," he thanked her by giving her a tin of pizzelles he made in the kitchen at St. John's.

"Tony and Peanut didn't raise a fool, and I owe it to them not to talk like one," he told her the next day when he dropped off the cookies.

The example comes to mind only because I looked like a flaccid fool when the guard at Toms River told us the truck from Bordentown had been turned away.

"All our existing waste cells have been capped and our expansion project won't be finished until next week," he said after Dupe explained our quest. "For the last month, garbage that normally is dumped here has been diverted to other collection centers."

When Dupe asked him the locations of the other collection centers, his answers made all the cells in my knees buckle and my mouth go dry.

"Around the state." "Around the country." "And maybe even around the world."

Then he started spouting statistics about trans-oceanic shipments of electronic waste, rusted ships and hazardous chemicals.

I tried to speak, but no words came out – in English or in PAL. As my whole body began to wobble, Dupe grabbed me by the collar of my shirt and pulled me upright.

"Personally, son, I think it's time to forget about your can   You'll be able to remember your past just fine without whatever's inside it," he said. "It's your business, though. If you want to keep looking, you can't let a few setbacks get you down.

"Tomorrow's a brand new day, and every new day brings a new chance to find what you're searching for."

But I couldn't look for my CANN the next day. The next day I wouldn't be looking for anything but my desk.

I was going to work!

Chapter 8
The education of an extraterrestrial

During the last six years at the *Star-Ledger*, I've held jobs beginning with every letter of the alphabet. From assistant swimming coach at the Armidale middle school in Sidney, Australia (perfect for an alien with gills!), to Zamboni driver at the Highland Ice Arena in St. Paul, Minnesota.

Some of what was in between A and Z wouldn't surprise you. Like travel agent, or jet mechanic, or planetarium guide. Exactly the kinds of positions you'd expect from a trans-galactic trekker.

But many of my experiences would fascinate you. Not because I'm an alien, but because, as Dupe said, they gave new meaning to the term "odd jobs." Like yawn counter at a sleep clinic, dinosaur bone duster at a museum, or snake milker in a pharmaceutical lab.

Snake
by Dr. J.J.

The list also includes drawbridge tender, high-rise window washer, cruise ship pianist, process server, male dancer at a ladies-only nightclub, wallpaper peeler, water tower painter, chimney sweep, bounty hunter, repo man, secret shopper, forest fire lookout, dog catcher, and more than 110 other occupations.

I've even written fortunes for a cookie company. My favorite was: *Beginning tomorrow, you will stop procrastinating.*

At first I looked for jobs in locations along the trail to my CANN. But no matter where I went, the story was the very same: The environmental waste recycling shipments from Newark had never arrived or had been sent somewhere else.

Apparently paint cans, brake fluid containers and computer screens travel almost as much as commercial airline pilots.

After my column was syndicated, jobs from around the world came looking for me. You name it, you can pretty much bet I've done it.

A year ago, the newspaper held a surprise party for me in honor of my 100th "Last Day on the Job." It turned out to be a double surprise because, after I walked into the newsroom, I realized I had decorated the cake for the celebration.

It was in a big white box on Frank Devereaux's desk, with "Congratulations on your new jobs" in bright green script across the lemon-yellow frosting. When I saw it I understood why the instruction, "Be sure 'jobs' is plural," had been triple-underlined in red on the order slip at Desio's, where I was a baker at the time.

I mention the surprise party only so you'll appreciate that during my time on Earth, I've done a lot of things, been a lot of places, and met a lot of people.

I've also learned a lot of stuff. About being a man. Happiness. Cooking. Courtesy. Economics. Entertaining. Philosophy. Investing. Marketing. Decorating. Sales. Poker-playing.

And acting, of course.

In all modesty, I don't think Marlon Brando himself could have portrayed a Paladino any better than I portrayed an earthling. He certainly could have been a contender, though.

I've learned about plenty of other subjects, too. But I'll save all those chronicles for another time.

What I want to tell you now is what I learned about being human. In my opinion, it's the most important story of all.

The difference between a human and a zibizzibiz is similar to the difference between your life and the life of Jimmy Malone's black lab, Research.

Resa, as everybody calls her, is a lucky dog. She's well cared for by the Malones. She has plenty of food and water; lives in a nice, warm house; is taken for a walk every afternoon; hangs out on the weekend with other dogs at the bark park; and goes on vacation with her owners twice a year.

She's happy, even though she doesn't get to choose what she eats or where and when she goes. Those decisions are made for her by humans.

Doesn't that sound like my life on Paladin?

Plenty to eat and drink; a comfortable apartment; happy hour on my balcony every afternoon; contact with associates at work; regularly scheduled vacations and supply trips.

I didn't get to choose my job, my travel destinations or my housing. Those decisions were made for me by the government. I was satisfied, because I didn't know any different or better.

But if you have a pet, you know that Resa's life includes a few extras that a Paladino's doesn't. Countless times a day she's praised for being a "good girl, good girl." She's petted, patted, scratched, smooched, cuddled, nuzzled and hugged. And every night she sleeps on top of the covers at the foot of Mama Rosa's bed.

Paladinos don't give or receive affection.

They never touch.

And they always sleep alone.

Resa's life is richer than a Paladino's. And a human's life is richer than Resa's.

If yours isn't, maybe what I'm about to tell you will help make it so.

It boils down to this:

1.) Humans have hearts that not only circulate blood, but also provide the capacity to experience emotion. Affection and attraction, compassion and mercy, sadness and sorrow, pleasure and desire. If you have no feeling in your fingers, your four other senses can help compensate. But if you can't feel with your heart . . . well, you just can't be human.

2.) Paladinos have big brains but, off the job, little to think about. What's the point of questioning your beliefs or behaviors if you don't have the ability to alter any aspect of your existence? It can only lead to dissatisfaction and frustration. But humans have the power to use their heads to changes their lives. On your planet, intellect is instrumental to happiness, not incidental.

3.) A Paladino's existence is planned, programmed and plotted like a Broadway play. Humans, however, can quite literally do exactly as they please because life on Earth is full of options and alternatives. You can even choose not to choose, if that's your preference. The decision to take control of your life doesn't make you a control freak; it makes you a human.

In KISSeR terms: *Feel. Think. Do.*

Believe me, you can.

Because you were born human. Naturally.

Me? I had to work at it.

In theory, a Paladino learning to be human should be about as natural as a giraffe learning to somersault.

But when you're blessed with a best friend who could teach a toddler to tango – and you have mirror neurons to boot – it's easier than you might expect.

That's why I start each lesson by describing what I learned from Dupe. Every hour with him is like sitting through an entire Ph.D. class in humanity.

I'm 100 percent earthling now. And there's no going back.

Even with a CANN.

Learning

Lessons for being human

✓ Love someone

✓ Love something you do

✓ Appreciate your parents

✓ Be kind

✓ Exercise your free will

✓ Take care of your health

✓ Keep growing

✓ Use your brain

✓ Believe in something bigger than yourself

✓ Eat sardines

Chapter 9.1
Love someone

I. What I learned from Dupe about loving ... *everyone*

As I've told you, a Paladino's emotions are completely impersonal. They result from situations and are directed at inanimate objects.

Such as:

I'm so excited about my new Cassegrain reflecting telescope, my head feels as if it's going to spin off into outer space.

Or:

If I bump my head on that Kapton sunshield one more time, it'll be the *$!#@! telescope, not me, that sees stars.

Until I came to Earth, I'd never experienced warmth, affection, fondness or even friendship. Those feelings are caused by and directed at people.

Not long after being trapped on your planet, things started to change. Dupe and my mirror neurons were the reason.

Dupe's as full of feelings as the ocean is of salt. He's always hugging, patting, pecking and touching the people he likes, which as far as I can tell is just about everyone.

Because we were together every day, I spent a lot of time watching him pat and peck. The next thing I knew, my mirror neurons had me doing the same. Peanut, Tony, Mighty Minnie, Mama Rosa, Jimmy, Angie, John and Phil all became recipients of my hugs and kisses – on the cheek, of course. Mr. Devereaux and Mrs. Rosenblatt, too.

And the *next* next thing I knew, the physical actions started producing chemical reactions.

I really *liked* these people.

A Paladino with feelings? The concept was completely foreign to me at first. No pun intended.

But now, it seems as normal as heartburn at a chili fest.

The tin man from the Wizard of Oz followed the yellow brick road to the Emerald City to get his heart. I found mine on Mulberry Street in Newark.

I take it with me everywhere I go. And, like Tony Bennett, I leave a little piece of it behind every place I visit, with every person I meet. If your heart is big enough – as mine is now – there's plenty to go around. Even if you're a world traveler like me.

Maybe this sounds a little crazy, but I even try to *see* with my heart. It picks up on things that my eyes and my brain can't. And it saves me from having to wear rose-colored glasses, which I'd probably accidentally sit on or lose.

It feels good to feel. In fact, maybe it's time for me to start watching love stories on DVD.

Casablanca tonight. Romance tomorrow?

II. What I learned on the job about loving someone

Working in the water is to me what being on the cover of a fashion magazine is to a model.

It just doesn't get any wetter, I mean better, than that.

I was a boat-hull cleaner for Tyte Scrapes, which is owned by Tealy and Taylor Tyte. Tealy happens to be Mr. Devereaux's daughter. When she called to tell him she was taking a leave the last month before her baby was born, he assigned me to fill in at the family business.

It was on the island of Oahu, in Hawaii. Which I'm sure you know is surrounded by the Pacific Ocean. Which you might not know is the largest body of water on Earth.

Talk about paradise.

I worked with Nakoa Akuna, a native who's the closest thing I've ever seen to a human fish. He couldn't stay underwater as long as I could, but then he doesn't have gills on his insteps.

On my first day, we were working on a 23-foot 1940 Chris-Craft Barrel-Back Runabout. It was a beauty. We had used long-handled floor scrapers to remove hundreds of barnacle bodies from the varnished mahogany bottom. Then we switched to paint scrapers to dislodge the husks.

After two hours, I understood why Nakoa was so lean and muscular. But not how Tealy could handle the job. She was a petite five-foot-two and, when she wasn't eight months pregnant, weighed only 100 pounds soaking wet.

The cool water was great, but the labor was more physically demanding than swinging a 20-ounce roofing hammer for eight hours a day. Which I'd done the previous year for a Fort Lauderdale contractor.

Paint scraper
by Dr. J.J.

When lunchtime finally arrived and Nakoa invited me to join him for lau-lau and rice at his house, I was so tired I couldn't wait to get back on dry land.

On the way, he told me about his wife, Halia. She had contracted encephalitis 18 years ago, just six months after they were married. The swelling of her brain caused one of the worst cases of amnesia in recorded medicine.

He said her motor skills, language, and general intelligence were fine. But her long-term memory had been completely wiped out, and her short-term memory lasted only a few seconds. She could take care of herself, but wouldn't remember brushing her teeth or drinking a cup of coffee immediately after she finished.

When we walked in the front door, she asked who we were. Nakoa took her in his arms, gave her a kiss, and explained that he was her husband and I was his friend. He heated the food left over from the previous night's dinner and we sat at the dining table, where he caressed his wife's arm with one hand and ate with the other. During the next 45 minutes, she asked who we were more than 15 times.

This was his life, and had been for almost two decades. If he told her 40 times a day that he was her husband – which seemed conservative – he had given 255,520 explanations by now. I almost wished Paladinos didn't have the aptitude for math that allowed me to calculate the total in my head.

I thought about how impatient I became when the Spanko twins asked me over and over and *over* why I always wore sandals and socks. Maybe my reaction to them had to do with my fear of being detected, but I didn't think so.

I glanced at Nakoa. He was nuzzling his wife's neck. As we left, she thanked us for coming and said she hoped she'd see us again one day.

When I asked Nakoa how he did it, he told me it was simple.

"Loving her keeps my heart beating. We took a vow to stay together in sickness and health, for better or worse. She didn't do this to *me*. This was done to *her*.

"When my heart aches, it aches for my beautiful bride, not for me. I can still scrape barnacles and compare today's sunset with yesterday's and remember that I'm married and in love. But my Halia can't do any of those things.

"She doesn't have a real life, even with me. But I do, and I couldn't have it without her."

Then he said something that has stuck with me like few other things I've learned on Earth.

"Never forget that a house is simply where you live. A home is where you love."

My home now is Newark, New Jersey, United States of America, Planet Earth.

And I love it here.

I haven't forgotten what I said about the city being full of people with big hair, big personalities and big mouths. But I was a pretty superficial tourist back then, interested only in grocery transactions, not human connections.

It didn't take me long to realize that Newark natives have big hearts, too.

I should have known that you can't test the temperature of a pool by sticking your toe in the shallow end. You have to dive right in.

Once I looked below the surface and got to know the place and its residents, I came to a surprising conclusion: I'd be a fish out of water anywhere else.

The people I've met here aren't just friends, they're family. We share happy occasions, sad moments, and fun activities with one another.

Next week 32 of us, including Peanut and Tony, are getting together at the Malones for Thanksgiving dinner. I'm in charge of sweet potatoes, so I'm perfecting my recipes.

One version will be whipped with maple syrup and walnuts and presented in individual, hollowed-out orange halves. The other will be smoked and served with a bourbon-cinnamon-Tabasco glaze.

I can't cook like Peanut and Mighty Minnie, but I enjoy experimenting in the kitchen. Preparing food that makes others smile is my way of thanking them for caring about me.

Newark isn't my home away from home any more. Newark is just plain home.

It's where I live and where I love, and it always will be.

Newark or nowhere.

Chapter 9.2
Love something you do

I. What I learned from Dupe about loving something you do

You might think that talking is what Dupe enjoys most in life. Or maybe taking naps. He's awfully good at both.

But if you want to see Dupe happier than an evangelist at Easter time, watch him at a piano.

He plays for nursing homes, wedding receptions, dances, and the occasional night club. He can't pass a keyboard without making music.

"Most kids hate lessons," Dupe told me. "But I loved them from the beginning. Once I learned Chopin's Etude in E Major, Opus 10, No. 3, my instructor, Mrs. Nestlewhite, said there was nothing more she could teach me.

"By the way, if that particular piece doesn't stir your soul, then you have embalming fluid, not blood, running through your veins."

Call me Pavlov's dog, but his reference to embalming fluid made my gills tighten up. Those are two words I'd be very happy never to hear again.

When Dupe was sitting at a piano, he was like a different person. No talking. No figuring. Almost no breathing. It was hard to tell where the instrument ended and Dupe began.

One day we saw a vendor at a corner pretzel stand try to shortchange a blind teenager. Dupe stopped him and said he'd better never hear of the man stealing from any more children, old ladies, or wounded veterans.

Dupe rarely gets angry. But when he does, his dark brown eyes look like two fiery embers that could burn a hole right through your skull. And his biceps and pectoral muscles swell with infuriation to the point where you're sure they'll burst his shirt wide open.

On the whole, he can be pretty intimidating when he's upset.

The pretzel seller apparently shared my opinion. He shrugged his shoulders at the rebuke, said, "Sorry, mate, it won't happen again," and handed the teen an extra $5.

"Maiale del diavolo," Dupe muttered as we crossed the street.

I happen to know that the exact translation is "devil pig," but Dupe said it meant "heartless blood-sucker."

He was clearly agitated as we walked. A block later, we entered the front door at A Capella Music.

Dupe greeted the fellow behind the counter with a "hey there, Gus," pulled out the bench in front of a Fazioli concert grand, and began to play.

During the 20 minutes we were there, his notes transitioned from stormy to sorrowful to serene. Then he stood up, pushed the bench back under the piano, and thanked Gus for the therapy session.

"When Congreve said music soothes a savage breast, he knew what he was talking about. A little Beethoven makes everything seem right with the world. Even if it really isn't.

"Find your oxygen, son. Music is mine. I don't need it to survive, but I sure need it to live."

I wasn't sure what Dupe meant at the time. But I understood later.

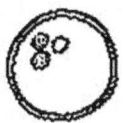

Bowling ball
by Dr. J.J.

I found my oxygen. On a chilly winter day in Las Vegas, Nevada, at the Lucky Strikes Lanes.

I can't say I live to bowl. Or that I bowl to live.

But I can tell you that nothing in the world – or even the universe – is more thrilling to me than the sound of my 16-pound, red, Roto-Grip Epic Odyssey ball scattering 10 hard-rock-maple pins across a waxed deck.

It's music to this alien's ears.

And when I'm surrounded by friends who chime in with a loud chorus of cheers after every frame, I realize that I struck it very lucky, indeed, the day I lost my CANN.

II. What I learned on the job about loving something you do

It was a Saturday in mid-August, the air a heavy cloak of suffocating heat and humidity. The luminous butterscotch moon hung low, silhouetting the leafy tree branches against a sky that was a contusion of black and blue. In the crowded stands, jiggly, fat women and scrawny, rawboned men, the whole of them tattooed and in tank tops, belched thick clouds of cigarette smoke into the lungs and eyes of all on the surrounding benches. Epithets were hurled, fingers were flipped, and the entire arena throbbed with fan loyalty gone rabid.

Welcome to race night at Bowman Gray Stadium, NASCAR's longest-running weekly track. It's two miles off Interstate 40 in Winston-Salem, North Carolina – home of Reynolds-American Tobacco, the first Fourth of July celebration in the United States, and Krispy-Kreme Doughnuts. The lap record of 55.283 miles per hour at the quarter-mile unbanked asphalt oval is still held by Richard Petty, nicknamed "The King" and widely considered the greatest NASCAR driver of all time (with apologies to Dale Earnhardt).

OK, OK, I know. Purple prose. Make that magenta.

But every once in a while it feels good to break free of KISSeR's handcuffs.

Anyhow, as I was saying . . . .

Funnel cake
by Dr. J.J.

I was in a concession trailer behind the bleachers, filling in for a fellow orderly at Wake Forest University Baptist Medical Center who was driving to Myrtle Beach for the weekend to get married. The trailer was owned by Betty Sue and Billy Joe Bedner, whose son, Junior, was racing for the Sportsman championship in the final event of the season.

Junior and another driver, Lonnie Davis, were so close together in points, whoever won the race would also take home the season trophy.

It was an easy night. Except for trying to resist the funnel cakes.

In less than five minutes, Betty Sue taught me to make them. She had a broken wrist, so she ran the cash register while I prepared the orders.

They're literally a piece of cake to cook: Put your finger over the end of a funnel. Pour a cup of pre-made batter into the top. Hold the funnel over a vat of hot oil. Release your finger. As the batter runs out in a stream, move your hand back and forth above the oil to make a pattern – circles, sticks, spirals or, if you're artistically inclined, try flowers and animals. Fry two-and-a-half minutes. Remove with a slotted spoon. Drain. Top with powdered sugar or honey.

Funnel cakes
(small batch)

| 1 egg | 2/3 cup milk | 2 tbsp. sugar |
| 1 1/4 cup flour | 1/4 tsp. salt | 1 tsp. baking powder |

Directions:
1. In a deep skillet, heat two cups of oil over medium-high heat until hot. Test the temperature by dropping a pinch of flour into the hot oil. If it sizzles right away without smoking, it's perfect.
2. Beat egg and milk. Mix all other ingredients in a separate bowl and slowly add to the egg mixture, beating until smooth.
3. Using a funnel, drop into hot oil, working from the center outwards in a web pattern. (You can use a gallon-sized freezer bag instead of a funnel by pouring the batter into the bag, snipping off a small corner, and squeezing the batter through the hole into the oil.)
4. Cook 2-3 minutes till golden brown and crispy.
5. Remove from oil. Sprinkle with powdered sugar or drizzle with honey and serve piping hot

---

A cinch for me to cook. An even bigger cinch for me to eat.

Junior burst through the back door just as I was moaning, groaning and wondering whether an overstuffed stomach could actually explode He was carrying a still-corked bottle of Korbel champagne and grinning like a Cheshire cat.

"I won, Mama. I won," he said, picking up Betty Sue and dancing the two of them around in a circle.

"Oh, sugar," she screeched. "Oh, sugar, that's just wonderful. I had the jitters and jumps so bad, I couldn't watch.   My fingers were crossed as tight as two shoelaces at a track meet."

The match-up between Junior and Lonnie had come down to the last turn of the last lap. It looked as though Lonnie would win, but when a competitor rammed his rear bumper, he spun into the wall at turn three.

Junior cruised   across   the finish line to the wave of the checkered flag and the roar of the crowd.

Betty Sue told me that Junior made a living by working with his father as a plumbing contractor. But on 16 Saturday nights every April through August, he lived his dream.   Tires cost him $800, a driver's uniform $1,500, and a new motor $25,000.   Year after year after year, for 12 years. He'd won 47 races with total prizes of less than $15,000 and two championships with winners' purses of $12,000.

> **Speaking of driving**
>
> I work in a lot of towns without public   transportation   –   no subways, taxicabs or even buses. When I told Dupe I didn't have a license or know how to drive, he said having chauffeurs was one thing, but my parents took the concept of the idle rich to new heights.   I enrolled in the No Crash Course taught by Russell "Rusty" Carr, who made the sign of the cross at the start of each lesson and, just minutes into my 30   hours   of   behind-the-wheel instruction, developed a severe eye tic that is with him to this day. For   someone   accustomed   to traveling around as canned vapor, I think I did pretty well. But Mr. Carr seemed awfully glad to put me in his rear-view mirror. If I wave at him when I'm driving around   town   these   days,   he doesn't wave back. I blame the eye tic, because it's practically impossible   to   miss   my   bright yellow 1958 Corvette Roadster.

"He takes that little bit of prize money and turns it into a whole lot of memories," she said.

After Junior left to join his friends for a victory celebration, Betty Sue and I locked up the trailer and walked to the parking lot.

"I guarantee you, five minutes from now, it won't matter a bit to him that he won," she said. "The only thing he'll be thinking about is how he's going to make it through the next eight months till racing starts up again. My son's like a lost ball in high weeds when the season ends. Doesn't know where to go or which way to turn.

"Junior's had a fire in his belly for racing since he was a boy. He'd get on his daddy's tractor and pretend he was Pee Wee Jones speeding around the track in his Chevy. Winning, losing – it's all the same to him. Long as he's behind the wheel, he's smiling."

I had a fire in my belly that night at Bowman Gray. But it was caused by too many funnel cakes.

Junior reminded me of a Russian man I read about in the *Star-Ledger* who had collected more than a half-million pounds of bottle caps and stored them in a warehouse. When I told Dupe about what I'd read and shook my head in bewilderment, he offered a simple explanation.

"Son, a purpose is about what you need to do in life. A passion's about what you want to do. For the truly lucky, they're one and the same. But even when they aren't, I guarantee you'll be a whole lot happier if you have both."

I guess that's partly why Paladinos are travel addicts. The Commissioners of Occupational Placement and Security – we call them COPS – decide which of our career opportunities we'll accept, so most of us don't enjoy what we do. Because of that, we have to make time for doing what we enjoy.

But devotion? And drive?

It isn't that Paladinos purposely steer clear of those earthling concepts. They simply aren't standard equipment for us.

It used to puzzle me when Jimmy Malone said he loved being a firefighter. When Mighty Minnie declared that she woke up smiling every morning, thinking about what she was going to cook for dinner that night. Or when John Spanko told me that winning a tough criminal case made him feel as if he'd just returned from a two-week vacation.

But now I understand. Not all jobs are work.

Mine isn't. Or maybe, because I've had so many, I should say mine *aren't*.

Doing what you love is like having your own gas station. Your tank never gets empty.

If you want to help combat the energy crisis, figure out where you really *want* to go before you set out on your journey. Then you'll be able to map out the best way to get there.

Based on my own experience, you'll find yourself looking forward not only to arriving at your destination, but also to the trip itself.

Chapter 9.3
Appreciate your parents

I. What I learned from Dupe about appreciating your parents

As I've mentioned before, Paladinos don't have parents. We have antecedents. They provide the raw material required to produce new Paladinos.

If you're thinking, "but an antecedent is just something that comes before something else," you've got the picture.

I don't know my antecedents, and they don't know me. We all look the same, so we couldn't pick each other out in a room – crowded or otherwise.

So I never understood the concept of parents. Or children. Or parent-child relationships.

Until I met Peanut and Tony.

Dupe might not have fulfilled their dreams for him, but when he walked in their front door every Sunday afternoon in Little Italy, you would have thought he was a soldier home from war and they were supportive and steadfast pen pals who had written him every day.

Their apartment was filled with more affection than you'd find at the opening event at a five-year high school reunion.

The visits started with hugs and kisses. And ended with hugs, kisses and, invariably, a "thank you, Mama, thank you, Papa, for who you are and all you've done for me." In between was a lot of laughing, talking, arm-waving and eating. Lots and lots of eating.

I was included in it all.

I admit that, at first, the constant touching made me feel like a rabbit at a petting zoo. But like the animals who are paid for their patience in pellets, my tolerance was rewarded with mouthwatering masterpieces from Peanut's kitchen.

I don't know if the rabbits ever begin to enjoy being stroked, but I know that this Paladino did.   Every hug or kiss was so soothing to my gills, I could feel them relax in a limp line along my instep.

The first time I visited with Dupe, he told his parents I had left home because "he wants to lead a simple life, Mama, just like me."

"Simple, complicated – that's not important," Peanut said, cupping my face in her hands and standing on tiptoe so she could look in my eyes. "What's important is happiness. Be a happy man. When you're happy, you make your parents happy.

"My son could have had a better life, and heaven knows his Papa and I tried to help him. But he couldn't have been a better person. So I don't always understand the things he does? Even the Blessed Virgin herself sometimes didn't understand her son."

With that, she pecked my cheek, walked over to the stove, and pulled a steaming dish of baked ziti out of the oven. "Now, mangia," she said, shooing us toward the dining room.

From that moment on, I wanted parents almost as much as I wanted to find my CANN.

One day, on the train ride back to Newark, I asked Dupe why, if he loved Peanut and Tony, he refused to live the life they imagined for him.

"You're thinking about it all wrong, son," he replied. "I don't refuse their life. I choose my own. And that's exactly what they expected from me.

"They gave me everything I needed to live any kind of life I wanted. Self-confidence, self-esteem, self-reliance – that's all a kid needs to make his own way in the world.

"Sure, they had an idea, maybe even a dream, of the kind of future I'd choose. But they couldn't force it on me any more than you could force a bird to walk on stilts instead of fly. And they didn't try very hard, either.

"Birds fly because that's what makes them birds. I make my own choices because that's what Mama and Papa taught me to do. And I thank them for it every chance I get.

"I realize the situation with your parents is different. They weren't around much when you were growing up. Truth is, some folks are a whole lot better at making kids than they are at rearing them. But I guarantee you, even if they weren't any good, they did the best they could.

"Besides, if it weren't for them, you wouldn't be here to enjoy Mama's cooking every Sunday afternoon."

Dupe didn't know how right he was about my . . . parents . . . not being around when I was growing up. But he was also right that, without them, I wouldn't be around at all.

They didn't give me the self-confidence, self-esteem, self-reliance or love that Peanut and Tony so amply bestowed on their son. But they gave me life, and with it the chance to make of my existence – and myself – whatever I set my mind, my heart, and my shoulder to.

Choosing between that and never being born is easy for me: I'm glad I'm here. Especially now that I'm *here*.

I know lots of earthlings who might as well be from Paladin in terms of their parental legacies. If you're one of them, don't worry. We have some catching up to do, but we'll make it.

Together.

I promise.

And don't forget, Paladinos never lie.

II. What I learned on the job about appreciating your parents

If you ever get the urge to study human nature, take a shot at bartending.

You'll learn more in a week serving drinks than a college student learns in an entire semester of psychology courses.

I found that out for myself at the Mustang Bar, in Pony, Montana, population 100.

Mrs. Rosenblatt had discovered the place while on a Merry Widows' Wild West Territory Tales and Trails Tour. The bar has been around since the early 1900s, just after the town's boom days as a gold miner's camp went bust. The mottled brick walls are lined with dented pans, dusty sluice boxes, scarred saddles and other relics of the town's mining and ranching roots.

She enjoyed the "authoritatively authentic ambiance and atmosphere" so much that, after drinking a few ice-cold draft beers to quench her thirst on what she claimed – but the weatherman couldn't confirm – was the hottest day on record, she tried to talk the owner into opening a franchise near the *Star-Ledger*.

Parker Elliott declined, saying a place in Newark could have ambiance and atmosphere, but it wouldn't be authentic. He had no idea, however, just what, or *whom*, he was up against.

Some people say Mrs. Rosenblatt can be convincing. All people say she can be relentless.

She left the bar without a franchise, but with Elliott's reluctant agreement to let me work for him for a couple of months while the long-time bartender, Wink Wilson, recovered from heart surgery.

Most of the patrons are locals – loggers, miners and ranchers who think of the Mustang as their home away from home. They come in every afternoon to sit with their buddies and unwind from a long stretch out in the elements.

Cowboy hat
by Dr. J.J.

Once or twice a week, a carload of tourists wanders in, anxious for a 24-karat frontier-land experience. They form a gaggle of giggles behind a ringleader, who inevitably walks up to a table of regulars and asks if they're real cowboys.

In my opinion, the best reply came from Jake Barnes.

"I tell you what, little lady, you be the judge. When I say 'go,' start running for the door. If I can drop a lasso around your neck and tie your legs together with a wrap and slap before you get there, you'll have your answer."

When strangers arrive in a group, they're looking for a colorful story to tell back home. And, like the little lady and her friends, they don't mind being teased to get it.

But when a stranger walks in alone to the Mustang Bar in the tiny, out-of-the-way town of Pony, Montana, he's looking for something he hasn't been able to find anywhere else. He can't tell you what it is. He just knows he doesn't have it.

That's the way it was with Hinley Shaw. He strode in early one evening with the cool self-assuredness of a surgeon entering an operating room. But, as everyone there could have told you, despite his impeccable grooming, expensive clothes, and moneyed good looks, Hinley was an unhappy man.

After two double scotches, he started telling jokes. Bad ones.

"Where does a cowboy cook his meals?" he asked, turning around on his stool to face the table behind him.

When he didn't receive a reply, he said, "Why, on the range, of course."

He followed up by asking in a louder voice if anyone had "heard the one about the bankrupt rancher who didn't complain"? "He simply had no beef."

Then came the shouted, "Why'd the bowlegged cowboy get fired?" "Because he couldn't keep his calves together."

Some of the toughest fellows I've ever met in my life were in the bar that day. Guys who could cut through a 20-inch log in less than 15 seconds, or rope and brand a 250-pound calf in under 10.

Guys who leave other people alone, and expect other people to afford them the same courtesy.

But not a single one of them said a single word to the dapper city slicker who had gone from annoying to obnoxious in five short minutes.

They knew that Hinley, who probably had anything and everything money could buy, was a sad soul. Sitting alone, on a stool, in their bar, in their town. Wishing he were one of them.

Not so much wishing he were a cowboy. Just wishing he could be a man who was content being who he was.

Before he tested the limits of their understanding and restraint, I offered Hinley a scotch on the house and asked what he did for a living.

"Financial advisor," he said. "Best in the country in fact, according to Barron's magazine. Rated number one the last five years in a row."

Xjmohhw!! No more free drinks for him. In fact, he'd better leave a big tip. Big enough to buy a round for everyone in the place, including the bartender.

A financial advisor. At the time, I didn't know anything about investments. And still don't.

I did, however, know the secret to making conversation with most earthlings: Get them talking about themselves.

So I asked him what the worst investment a person could possibly make was.

I thought my question would challenge him. After all, he was used to talking to clients about good investments, not bad ones.

But he answered immediately.

"That's easy. It's children," he said with a rueful expression.

When I asked him to explain, he put a $100 bill on the bar and ordered another double.

"I work like a rented pack mule to take care of my family. And always have. Ballet, tap, piano, karate, tennis, guitar lessons . . . my son and daughter had them all when they were little.

"I spent endless hours at their recitals and games and competitions. Never missed a performance. I paid for bicycles and braces and birthday parties. In high school it was cars and cheerleading outfits and football uniforms.

"Now they're in the big leagues – private university tuition, parking passes, sorority dues, fraternity weekends and spring break trips.

"Thousands of dollars and thousands of hours invested in them. And what thanks do I get? Absolutely none, that's what.

"Last week I was in San Francisco on business. I called my daughter at Stanford and told her I'd like to drive to Palo Alto and take her to dinner.

"'Oh, Daddy, I'm sorry, but I can't,'" she said in a voice so sweet it nearly melted my heart. "It's the first Tuesday of the month.'

"What exactly does that mean, honey?" I asked her.

"'Oh, Daddy, it's Tri Delta's date function night. It's a t-shirts and tiaras theme and I can't miss it. I'm the social chairman.'"

He gave me a bleary-eyed look and drained his glass.

"It's one excuse after another," he said. "'Dad, I can't go fishing this weekend. The guys and I are taking a road trip to Florida.' 'Dad, I don't want to go on a family cruise this summer. A bunch of us are working at a resort in Jackson Hole.' 'Daddy, you simply can't expect me to give up my Aruba vacation. Everybody from school is going.'

"Apparently, only foolish old men think their children want to spend time with them. When my daughter turned me down for dinner, I called my wife and told her not to pick me up at the airport in the morning," he said. "I'm driving back to Atlanta instead. And I'm doing some hard thinking about my priorities along the way."

Speaking of colors

When I walked out of my bedroom one afternoon after getting dressed to take Angie's and John's sons to the Adventure Aquarium in Camden, Dupe stood up from his chair and snorted with laughter. "Well, if it isn't Mr. Roy G. Biv himself," he chortled. "You're wearing more colors today than the Dutch Boy has in his entire product line." Once he explained that Roy G. Biv was a mnemonic for the hues in a rainbow (red, orange, yellow, green, blue, indigo and violet) and that Dutch Boy was a paint brand, I was flattered, not insulted. In honor of our destination, I was wearing a pair of dark pink cotton pants embroidered with blue whales; a blue polo shirt with an alligator logo; an aqua needlepoint belt accented with yellow mahi-mahi; and a sweater striped in the shades of a sunset wrasse. Life on Earth is vibrant and stimulating, unlike the dreary drabness of life on Paladin. I want my clothes, my home, my flower garden and everything but my sandals and socks to look the way I feel – bright and cheerful. And I want to help others around me feel the same way. It's hard to be unhappy when you're surrounded by rainbows.

Here was a man on a quest for validation. He needed to know that his loved ones appreciated, or at least noticed, the sacrifices he had made on their behalf. He didn't want to believe it all had been in vain.

I thought of Peanut and Tony and everything they had done for Dupe. About Dupe's lifestyle and how different it was than the one his parents had hoped and planned for him.

I asked Hinley if his children were happy.

"Are they happy? Are you kidding me? Happy doesn't begin to describe it," he replied. "They have everything they could possibly want. They have a mother and father who would do anything in the world for them. They have old friends they've known since they were toddlers and new friends they've met in school.

"They're popular and good-looking and talented. Their professors love them because they're so smart. When they graduate, they'll have their pick of jobs. Why shouldn't they be happy?"

As soon as he uttered the last sentence, his expression changed from bitter consternation to utter comprehension.

"Good God, my man, you're a genius. An absolute genius," he said. "What in the world are you doing, stuck out here in the middle of nowhere?

"My children are, without a doubt, the happiest people I know. And that makes me very, very happy.

"Merciful God in heaven, why didn't I understand it sooner? I've been sitting here wallowing in self-pity, but my parents were in the very same situation. They did everything in the world for me, and I never appreciated it until this very moment. All my success in life, and I just realized that they made every bit of it possible.

"My achievements and happiness are the only thanks they ever expected or received. And given a choice between a word of gratitude from my children and their well-being, I'd choose the former, too.

"But there's no reason my mother and father can't have both. I need to catch a plane," he said. "Which way is the closest airport?"

Hinley Shaw came to Pony looking for something he hadn't been able to find anywhere else. But it turned out he could have saved himself the trip.

He'd been looking in the wrong places. The answer had been in his heart all along.

Sure, he was proud to be ranked number one, and he certainly enjoyed all the trappings of his wealth. But what he really, truly savored was knowing that his investment in his children had paid off.

Just as his own parents' had.

I don't think he would have traded that knowledge for all the gold in Fort Knox.

He did what he did out of love, with no strings attached and no expectation of financial return. Nevertheless, I hoped that, just as Hinley had realized the stake his parents had in his success, his own children would someday acknowledge the advantages he had given them.

Mostly I hoped that, unlike Hinley, they wouldn't have to travel to Pony, Montana, in order to do so.

As for me, I hurtled 12.5 million miles through the globasphere before I understood that, although my . . . parents . . . hadn't given me a head start in life, they'd given me a life.

And that, at least, was a start.

Chapter 9.4
Be kind

I. What I learned from Dupe about being kind

Everything I have on this Earth I owe to Dupe: a name, a job, a place to live, friends, hobbies, sardines. In fact, my very existence.

If I had tripped over someone else besides him in the alley, I probably wouldn't be here telling you my story today.

Most men would not react favorably to someone who wakes them up and then has nothing to say for himself except "bjzy swlin kpzg erlx rnlud mpzoi."

Most men would probably punch that someone in the nose.

I'm a tough Paladino. I'd punch back.

Most men who lived in Newark and had friends there would probably then yell for some of those friends to help him.

And they probably would.

The fight in the alley would probably attract the attention of a passerby, who would probably call the police.

The police would probably take me to jail. And once I got there, they'd probably tell me to strip down to my underwear.

Boxer shorts
by Dr. J.J.

Then they'd notice that I still had on my shoes and socks. No probably about it.

They'd probably order me to remove them. I'd definitely refuse.
They'd probably try to take them off for me.

Then the real trouble would begin.

I'd kick my legs all over the place as if my life depended on it.
Which it would.

When it was all over, my gills would be revealed. And instead of
enjoying a long life as a dynamic, breathing creature, I'd spend an
endless future as a bunch of inert, floating puzzle pieces in a chemistry-
class container.

On the day Dupe befriended me in the alley, he saved my life. He
didn't know I was an alien, but he knew I was alone and afraid. That
was enough for him.

I probably don't have to say anything else about Dupe's kindness,
do I?

Before I came down to Earth, I never considered anyone else's point
of view, position, or predicament. I never considered anyone else,
period.

And no one else ever considered me.

"It's not my job." "It's not my problem." "That's not my concern."

On Paladin those aren't merely commonly used expressions, they're
universally held beliefs.

When you live on a planet where the government manages every
aspect of everyone's life, you end up thinking that no one is your
personal responsibility. And if you don't have to care *for* anyone, it's
easy not to care *about* anyone.

Here, though, earthlings look after – and look out for – each other.
It's contagious, too. Once people care about you, it's hard not to care
about them. And once you care about someone, you have to be
prepared to care about almost everyone.

That's what happened to me, anyhow. My feelings started with
Dupe, spread to Peanut and Tony, then grew to include Jimmy and
Mighty Minnie (Mama Rosa, too, of course). After that, I lost track.
Phil, Father Mo, Mr. Devereaux, Mrs. Rosenblatt, Angie and John . . .
and a whole long list of people I haven't mentioned yet. Or even met.

Now I carry in my back pocket my own small envelope made of two
Catholic prayer cards taped together on three sides. Inside is a

quote from Plato that reminds me to put myself in other people's sandals and socks . . . er . . . shoes when I interact with them.

"Be kind, for everyone you meet is fighting a hard battle."

Whether the battle is against illness, or financial problems, or stress, or the nagging doubts or relentless demons that live inside us, we're all engaged in some kind of minor or major daily struggle. Why would I make it worse for anyone by being unkind?

Besides, I don't want to take any chances. The next person I meet might be a terrified alien stranded in space and desperate to find his way home.

Stranger things have happened.

II. What I learned on the job about being kind

It was my day off from work as a lid tester at a peanut butter processing plant in Fitzgerald, Georgia, population 9,185. I was sitting in a booth at Shoney's, eating my way through a plate piled high with breakfast buffet food and skimming the local newspaper.

I write for the *Star-Ledger* but, because I'm out of town most of the time, I don't subscribe to it myself. However, I didn't have to be a regular reader to know that Newark's daily was as different from Fitzgerald's weekly as a meteor is from a mongoose.

The front page of the Herald-Leader in front of me contained no state, national or international news. The reporting was all local.

"City budget deficit tops $6,700." "Souper Sunday canned food drive kicks off this weekend."

And feature stories: "Local resident returns from tour of European castles." "New teams sign on for Relay for Life."

And editorials: "Mayor's policy WRONG!" "Police chief actions appropriate."

At the bottom of page three, a small notice in a black-bordered rectangle caught my eye. "Thank you to the man who helped me get up off the floor after I fell in the pet food aisle at Walmart. May God bless you, sir. Mrs. Violet Pettibone"

A simple act of kindness on the part of the unidentified man. A kind act of gratitude on the part of the woman he helped.

Georgia folks are like that. Not long after the end of the Civil War, when a drought destroyed crops across the Midwest, the battle-ravaged state was one of the first to send trainloads of supplies to help fellow Americans.

Shortly afterward, the city of Fitzgerald was founded as a Union soldiers' colony, just 10 miles from where Jefferson Davis, president of the Confederacy, had been captured. Settlers named the original streets after 14 generals and four battleships from the War Between the States – with equal numbers Union and Confederate.

Talk about not holding a grudge . . . .

Bag of dog food
by Dr. J.J.

On my first day in town, I was driving to the Piggly-Wiggly grocery store when I came to an intersection blocked by a police cruiser. A uniformed officer was outside the car, standing at attention next to the driver's door. Head high, eyes straight ahead, and hat over his heart.

As I watched, a shiny black hearse drove by, followed by a line of two dozen cars with their headlights burning.

"Police" and "permanently pickled in preservatives" are closely linked in my brain. But my curiosity got the better of me.

When the last car had passed and the officer waved on the line of waiting vehicles, I pulled next to him and asked what local dignitary had died.

"Dignitary? Why, we don't have many dignitaries in Fitzgerald, sir. And as far as I know, they're all still alive," he responded. "A 75-year-old woman named Julia Ann Nichols was in the hearse today. I don't know whether she was important in life. It doesn't matter. In this town we honor the departed. All of them."

I had seen funeral processions before. But only as I sped past in the other direction, relieved that I hadn't been caught behind the creeping column of cars. Never, though, had I seen opposing traffic come to a halt.

During the three or so minutes it had taken for the slow-moving motorcade to go by, no one honked a horn. Or squealed tires while making a quick U-turn. Or waved an impatient fist out an open window.

Hurrying, scurrying and worrying all stopped for the slightest sliver of time as everyone paused to show deference for the dead and consideration for the loved ones left behind.

When I described what I had seen to Helen Woods, my supervisor at the plant, she couldn't understand why I found the experience even worth mentioning.

"Those folks were just showing common courtesy, like their mamas taught them. 'Nice don't cost nothin'.' That's the Golden Rule, southern style," she

Speaking of talking

Some people find English complex and difficult to learn, partly because one word can mean so many different things and can be pronounced differently even when it's spelled the same. For example, "run" can be a noun, adjective, or verb, and has 150 different definitions. And I can think of at least 78 heteronyms, which are words that are spelled the same but are pronounced differently and have different meanings. Like "close" the door and a "close" race, or "bow" your head and put a "bow" in your hair. I don't care if the language makes sense. I'm content with the content because there's an English word or expression for everything you could possibly want to declare or describe. Some feel as good on the tongue as they sound to the ear: "hydrangea," "serendipity," "scintillating," and "effervescent." I also like "gizmo," "canoodle," "lollipop" and "cockamamie." And who doesn't enjoy saying, "he pounded the pavement" or "she was flying by the seat of her pants"? When it comes to verbal recreation, English is the bee's knees!

said. "Everybody learns it. Ought to, anyhow.

"You gotta give what you want to get back.   A smile.   An encouraging word.   A 'thank you.' It makes other people feel good, and it makes them feel good about you. But you want to know a secret? It makes you feel even better."

Helen was talking about earthly kindnesses that are costless to give, priceless to receive, and completely unheard of on Paladin. On a planet whose inhabitants don't have feelings for one another, there's no distinction between courtesy and cruelty. Paladinos say what they want without regard to whether it's helpful or hurtful. And our advanced critical thinking skills cause us to find problems with just about everything and everyone.

It isn't constructive criticism, because our intention isn't to make whatever it is better. In fact, we have no intention at all. Fault-finding is just what we do best.

For example, not too long after I arrived here, Phil asked Dupe and me what we though of the new logo for her real estate business. I had just read a story about Paya, the painting elephant, and replied that it looked like something a pachyderm would produce after a two-week drinking binge. I couldn't help it. It was the truth.

As you can imagine, Phil didn't take kindly to my opinion.

Luckily, I've since learned to *talk* positively, even if my brain doesn't always think that way. I care about people now, so I care about whether I hurt their feelings.

If Phil asked me about the same logo today, I'd say something like, "Your choice of fonts is perfect. But I'm not sure the images are crisp enough to be deciphered from the road. Also, the combination of a red house and a green spruce tree might be so strongly associated with the holidays that passersby will think of Christmas rather than of your company. If you paint the house gray with black shutters, it will stand out against the sign's white background without distracting from your name and phone number, which is what you want people to remember."

That's telling the truth with my head *and* my heart. And I do it now without even having to think.

It feels as natural as breathing. Through my gills.

Chapter 9.5
Keep growing

I. What I learned from Dupe about continuing to grow

Dupe has more hobbies than a centipede has feet.

He collected coins, comic books, baseball cards and bugs when he was a child. The insects died of natural causes, but it's still hard to imagine Dupe sticking a pin through them into display boards. He wouldn't hurt a fly.

Once he masters an endeavor, he moves on to another pastime. Right now he's into calligraphy, cake decorating, watercolor painting and woodworking. You should see the beautiful inlaid box he created for Tony's cutting knives. He's also teaching the members of a ladies' garden club the finer points of raising Brachypetalum-type lady slipper orchids.

Wedding cake
by Dr. J.J.

One day he and I were walking to a restaurant supply store to buy pastry bag tips he needed to decorate a wedding cake he was making for Angie's niece. On the way, he was talking to me – trying to, anyhow – about a book titled *Phenomenology of Sprit* and the ways in which Hegelian dialectic changed the formula for deductive reasoning.

I couldn't follow him. And frankly, I didn't want to. So I asked why he wanted to do and know about everything in the universe.

"Why, it's simple, son," he said. "When growth ends, decay begins. Once I quit being curious about the world and all it holds, I quit being interested in living. As far as I know, the only alternative to living is dying. And that's one subject that doesn't interest me at all."

Dupe doesn't have a college degree. But when it comes to being smart, he could write a textbook.

When I was on Paladin, my routine was really a rut. I worked; I sat on my deck every afternoon with a drink and a smoke; I traveled; I served time in the SEX RoOM.

I still work and travel. And I still sit on my deck occasionally, although I've found that a bird-watching book and a pair of binoculars help me relax far more than a glass of bourbon and a smelly cigar ever did.

But service in a procreation lab is a thing of the past. And so is the rut.

You never know what on Earth I'll be up to, or where on Earth I'll be.

Kayaking down North Carolina's New River. Taking a class in Weng Chun from Sifu Moy Yat. Attending the National Genealogical Conference in Charleston. Learning to fly fish at Henry's Fork in Last Chance, Idaho. Barbecuing a pizza on the grill in my back yard. Sailing on Lake Michigan. Inverting a matrix in a linear algebra course at Rutgers. Making the perfect pecan pie in my kitchen. Watching sunbathers at the Jersey shore. Skateboarding at the Louisville Extreme Park in Kentucky.

Maybe even signing up for an online dating service.

There's so much to do and so much to learn. I'll never run out of living.

II. What I learned on the job about continuing to grow

Annie Jane Johnson taught me to fly like a bird.

No, I didn't forget to tell you anything. Aliens don't have wings. If we did, I could have flown back to Paladino without my CANN.

Most humans don't have wings, either. But Annie Jane does.

She worked in a ticket booth outside the parking garage at Doctor's Hospital and Clinical Services in Albuquerque, New Mexico. I was in the booth next to her, just a car's width away.

Nowadays, health care facilities are as busy as the San Diego Freeway during rush hour. Car after car after car after car. In and out. In and out. In and out.

We only dealt with the outs. The people who were paying to leave.

Some of them were nice. They probably weren't very sick.

Some of them were mad. They probably had to wait too long to see someone.

And some of them were downright mean. They probably had just learned that they were very, very ill.

Annie Jane treated each and every one of them like a VIP.

You might not think that a parking attendant would have enough time to do that. But Annie Jane did. And even the maddest and the meanest lingered a little longer at the ticket booth to soak in her optimism and happy spirit.

One evening our shifts ended at the same time. I looked over and saw Annie Jane's cornrowed and beaded shiny black head disappear from the window of the booth. Seconds later, the door slid open and she rolled out on an oversized skateboard.

She had no legs.

She either didn't notice my shock or pretended not to. She smiled and invited me to join her for dinner in the hospital cafeteria. I agreed, and ambled beside her as she pushed herself along the sidewalk with leather-gloved hands.

Once inside, she put her palms on the seat of a chair and lifted herself up. The cashier came over to our table and, after introductions, Annie Jane ordered "the usual for Monday night."

As we ate, I told her about my *On the Job with Dr. J.J.* assignments, and she told me about her life.

She lost her legs when she was 17. She and her boyfriend were on their way to the senior prom when their car was struck by a drunk driver who ran a red light.

Her boyfriend was killed. She was hospitalized for six months. The drunk suffered only minor injuries.

I've mentioned more than once that Paladinos only get upset at situations, not at people. But I think that particular situation would be what earthlings call an exception to the rule.

"I work at Doctor's 20 hours a week to help pay my college tuition," Annie Jane said. "It's a great job. I talk to hundreds of people every day, and when I'm sitting up on my stool, none of them would guess that I'm any different than they are."

She pushed her plate to the side, clasped her hands together and said, "I've talked enough about myself. So, tell me, what do you do for fun?"

I named eating, swimming, bird watching, bowling and playing basketball. Traveling, too, of course.

Then I asked her the same question.

"Well, I'm a tournament bridge player, I can cook up a table full of soul food in no time flat, I make all my own clothes – you can imagine how difficult it would be to find pants to fit me, ha ha ha ha ha – I'm not bad on the clarinet, and I love hang gliding," she answered.

Hang gliding?

The confusion must have shown on my face.

"Just because I look like a tree stump doesn't mean I have to act like one," she laughed.

I apologized and told her I simply didn't understand how she did it.

"You really don't need your legs except for takeoff and landing," she said. "An engineer friend built me a special rig that's like a fancy pair of skis on mechanical shafts. They're attached to an aluminum frame and I control them with levers.

"I'll be honest: Getting airborne isn't easy. But it's worth the effort. And when I come down, it's like I'm landing on my own two feet. If my harness weren't so short, you'd never even know I'm a double amputee.

"I tell people that I might not be able to walk, but I sure can fly."

She said she knew a master pilot at the My Way is the High Way Hang Gliding School and would be happy to take me there on Saturday for a lesson.

I started stammering. Not because English isn't my first language.

Because I'm used to flying around in a nice, safe CANN. Hanging hundreds of feet above the ground from a flimsy frame sounded to me like persecution, not pleasure.

"You really ought to give it a try," she coaxed. "It's an incredible high."

Pun intended, I'm sure.

I told her I preferred to spend my Saturday afternoons on terra firma at the bowling alley.

"That's exactly why you should come with me. If you don't do something different now and then, your sense of adventure will die. And when that happens, you'll start getting old. Just like that," she said with a snap of her fingers.

"If anyone has an excuse for staying stuck in the same place, it's I. But since the accident I've learned that it doesn't matter how fast you go, or even how far you go, as long as you keep moving.

"I don't have legs. But I have wings. And if you'll come with me this weekend, you can have them, too."

When you're tall and two-legged, it's difficult to argue with someone who's neither. So I went.

I have to say that, once you get over the sheer terror, the view is incredible. And it's much more enjoyable than blasting through space at 37,000 miles an hour.

But I don't think I'll do it again. I'll try a different adventure instead. Maybe whitewater rafting.

Annie Jane was right. Growing older is a certainty, but growing old is a choice.

She was also right that, when you put your mind to doing something, the sky's the limit.

I have my mind – and my heart – set on landing an assignment as an astronaut. No one has more experience in outer space than I do, and once, just once, I'd like to make the trip into the stratosphere in something besides a CANN.

Awake, alert, and alive. It's the only way to fly.

Chapter 9.6
Use your brain

I. What I learned from Dupe about using your brain

One night, after he and I had finished a game of chess, Dupe headed to my back door to sleep outside on the porch, which he did several times a week. I offered him my guest bedroom, just as I had countless times before.

He refused. Just as he had every other time.

Not long after being stranded on Earth, I realized that my day-to-day life was normal. Not normal for a stranded alien, of course. Normal for an earthling.

I had a fulltime job, a rented duplex, and a well-stocked refrigerator.

A walk-in closet crammed with clothes, too. In fact, you might call me a fashion plate. I like Kasil jeans, Ed Hardy t-shirts, Armani suits and Deng Yin ties. I even own a Brioni tuxedo.

I bought them all at the Salvation Army.

I was an alien living an average earthling life. With the exception of my tuxedo. And Dupe was living a life that the average earthling would find alien.

In fact, Mrs. Rosenblatt looks at Dupe sideways every time she sees him – the way he first looked at me when I tripped over him in the alley. She describes his lifestyle as "unambiguously unconventional," but says she has to admit that, as a person, he's "curiously charismatic."

I decided that this would be the night I'd ask Dupe whether he was bothered by people's opinion of his strange habits. His answer was mind-boggling.

"Let me right quick ameliorate, assuage and attenuate your angst, anxiety and apprehension. Being bothered, bedeviled, beset or burdened by the conjectures, conclusions, consensuses or contentions of a determined, dogged and diligent denomination of detractors is foolish, feeble-minded and, furthermore, futile. Guarantee herewith, I implore, that any jabberwocky that kids, ladies, men or nincompoops opine pursuant to questions raised by those seeking total understanding of my various weirdnesses will be yielded zero attention.

"Zip! Zilch!

"And just in case you were wondering, son, I skipped the 'e's on purpose. I always found them kind of evil-looking, sitting there like clamshells with eyes."

I felt like a clamshell myself after he finished. Mouth agape and eyes agog.

Obviously, I've been doing a little vocabulary-building, too.

But the fact that he could string all those words together like beads on a bracelet . . . well, it astonished me more than seeing a tiny Asian woman eat 14 hot dogs at the Idaho state fair.

"That's what happens when you turn off the TV and turn on your brain," Dupe said. "It's the easiest part of your body to exercise. You can do it sitting down without ever breaking a sweat.

Speaking of clothes

In the library with Dupe one day, I read a magazine article in which Fonzworth Bentley, host of the MTV series *From G's to Gents*, gives men 10 tips on dressing well. I've checked off eight of the suggestions on his list: I own a three-piece suit; a corduroy jacket; dress shirts in blue, white, pink, lavender, check and stripe; a black turtleneck; a rack of terrific ties; an alligator belt (apologies to exotic-animal lovers and PETA members, but I prefer hide from aquatic creatures); pants that are always around my natural waist and that break exactly right; and I have a tailor who could custom-fit a hospital gown. I skipped the fashionable umbrella (people with gills want to stay *in* the rain, not out of it) and bench-made shoes (even sandals feel too restrictive on my feet). Whether I'm wearing something on Mr. Bentley's top-10 list or a less traditional, more colorful selection of my own, I think I fit the definition of a dandy. Even in my sandals and white socks.

"Most people want to take their mind off things. I want to put mine on. I stretch it till it just about hurts. Otherwise, it might shrink up on me. If I'm ever going to learn to play Schumann's Toccata in C Major, I have to keep my fingers *and* my brain flexible."

Dupe was implying that even a genius – like Leonardo DaVinci or Sir Isaac Newton – might just as well have the intelligence of an egg yolk if he doesn't put his mental capacity to work.

It makes a lot of sense, if you think about it.

After I wrote a computer program to handle the heavy statistics associated with my work as a retrocession actuary on Paladin, the job was a real no-brainer. The biggest challenge was staying awake.

Bō-ring.

That's the way it is for most Paladinos. Because of our high IQs, just about anything we do quickly becomes ho-hum humdrum.

For the most part, we're content to keep our brains on idle. We watch a lot of STOP-and-SIT, which stands for Spontaneous Thought-Originated Programming and Synchronized Interactive Technology.

It's similar to TV, except there are no networks or stations broadcasting live or taped shows. Instead, we wear special helmets that allow us to see images of our own thoughts, instantaneously produced in the form of holograms.

Whatever we can imagine, we can view. And because the helmets contain transceivers, we can synchronize our thoughts with those of other Paladinos to generate fully interactive optical impressions. We can also turn off the helmet's cranial scanning feature and simply watch someone else's mental concoctions. As long as the envisioner selects the multiple viewers option.

You can imagine how addictive STOP-and-SIT is. I watched an average of four hours a day. That's way on the low end for Paladinos.

In fact, GET OUT, which is shorthand for Government Education Targeted at Obsessive Use of Technology, is one of the biggest and most expensive counteroffensive measures on the planet.

Producing "programs" with plots and casts of characters requires creative thinking. After you've done it a few times, though, the process becomes heavier on the creative than on the thinking.

To borrow an earthling expression, we can do it with our eyes closed. Literally, of course.

Some of the best jobs I've had on Earth were the ones that forced me to shift my brain out of neutral and put it in gear.

Like serving as a crypto-linguist on a USAF RC-135V/W RIVET JOINT plane. The aircraft are equipped with all kinds of sophisticated intelligence-gathering equipment for monitoring coded electronic activity.

Crypto-linguists are code breakers with a twist: the code is written in a foreign language. In my case, it was Sidamo, an Afro-Asiatic dialect belonging to the Cushitic sub-phylum.

Getting the assignment was almost impossible because it required a security clearance. If Mr. Devereaux hadn't called his friend the New Jersey senator, and if I hadn't just been dubbed by *People* magazine as the "World's Most Brilliant Bachelor" after winning $4,270,500 on "Jeopardy!," I probably wouldn't even have been considered.

I can't tell you what I heard or saw or did on the job. That's Top Secret. What I can tell you is that, once the assignment was over, my brain was in such good shape, I deciphered the Egyptian Hieroglyphic, Egyptian Demotic and Greek inscriptions on the Rosetta Stone in less than a week.

It was an exercise in sheer, mind-bending recreation!

II. What I learned on the job about using your brain

Paladinos don't have pets.

They don't have feelings for one another. How in the world could they have feelings for a frog or a fish or a parakeet or a poodle?

But I have feelings now. And I want a dog. A Labrador retriever, Irish water spaniel or some other breed that loves to swim almost as much as I do.

It wouldn't be fair to the pooch, though. I travel too much.

So I did the next best thing. I got a job as a dog walker.

Wag 'n' Train Pet Obedience and Sitting Services, in Stow, Ohio, had 250 customers who owned 313 dogs. I was responsible for exercising four of them, three times a day, five days a week.

I could tell you tails of being dragged around by a bounding, barking pack of hounds determined to sniff, lick and chase anything and everything they see. Some outings can be downright ruff, to put it mildly.

Dog leash
by Dr. J.J.

Lulu Weaver made it look like a stroll in the park.

I met her at Bow Wow Beach, a seven-and-a-half-acre fenced-in area along Silver Springs Lake. Her twin Doberman pinschers paced side-by-side just ahead of her, as unflappable as the Honor Guard I saw last summer at the Tomb of the Unknown Soldier.

Lulu's a human encyclopedia – a know-it-all in the truest sense of the term.

She always talked aloud as she walked. Dogs are wonderful companions, but they aren't known for their conversational skills. So I first suspected that Lulu might be a stranded alien just like me who had lost her CANN – or other mode of travel – somewhere in the park. I speculated that she constantly repeated the name of her planet as she walked in the hopes of coming close enough to be whisked back home.

One afternoon, as my canine quartet pulled me across the grassy knoll where Lulu was standing, I listened as hard as I could to what she was saying.

". . . . The cold queen of England is looking in the glass; The shadow of the Valois is yawning at the Mass; From evening isles fantastical rings faint the Spanish gun, And the Lord upon the Golden Horn is laughing in the sun . . . ."

Hmmm. That didn't sound like the name of a planet to me.

On our next pass, I heard:

"'Stewardesses' is the longest word typed with only the left hand. The only 15-letter word that can be spelled without repeating a letter is 'uncopyrightable.' Wilma Flintstone's maiden name was Wilma Slaghoople. Betty Rubble's maiden name was Elizabeth Jean McBricker.

"The letter combination 'ough' can be pronounced nine different ways. 'A rough-coated, dough-faced, thoughtful ploughman strode through the streets of Scarborough; after falling into a slough, he coughed and hiccoughed.'"

I decided to approach her and ask what her walk-and-talk routine was all about.

Lulu greeted me with a great big smile. Animal lovers tend to be very friendly. Even if their pets aren't.

Her dogs greeted me with protective growls. Thankfully, the snarling ended immediately after a silent signal from Lulu.

She explained what she referred to as her symbiotic strategy.

"The sound of a human voice is soothing to animals. So I learn facts I can recite to my dogs, Planck and Maxie," she said. "Rote memorization is also good for my concentration and focus. And it requires no thinking whatsoever."

Dupe liked to be thinking all the time. Analyzing. Evaluating. Intellectualizing.

Trying to stop his wheels from turning would be like trying to stop a rooster from crowing at sunrise.

When I wondered aloud why Lulu didn't want to think, she set me straight.

"I'm a physicist studying Lorentz invariant intrinsic decoherence. If you have no earthly idea what that is, don't worry. Only a few hundred people in the country have a clue.

"At work, I'm always thinking. And I love it. There's nothing more satisfying than solving a perplexing problem. It's like running a marathon. When you cross the finish line, you're exhausted and exhilarated at the same time.

"But I need to relax my brain every once in a while. Memorizing poetry and speeches and trivia and historical facts and everything else I read makes me feel like a ballerina at the barre, limbering up my muscles for the next performance.

"Your mind can take you places your body can't go. But only if you keep it in shape."

Hearing Lulu describe the way she practiced memorization to unleash her problem-solving potential made my doggone head hurt.

Stretching your brain to help relax your brain. It's one trick I still haven't been able to learn.

Why not? Because I picked a pastime that can occasionally be extremely frustrating.

Solving riddles.

There's nothing relaxing about being unable to figure out the answer to one of those deceptively simple, cleverly contrived questions.

Dupe got me started the day he casually asked, "What's black when you buy it, red when you use it, and white when you're through with it?"

We happened to be standing over a grill at the time, flipping hamburgers at the Boys and Girls Club annual softball tournament, so it didn't take me more than a second to realize it was charcoal.

That was all it took to make me flip over riddles.

Like this one:

A man is in a room that has no windows or doors and contains nothing but a mirror and a table. How can he get out?

Answer: He should look in the mirror and see what he saw. Take the saw and cut the table in half. Two halves make a hole. Crawl out the hole.

Or how about this one:

If I say to you, "Everything I tell you is a lie," am I telling you the truth or a lie?

Answer: A lie. If it's the truth, then the statement itself is inconsistent with my claim that everything I say is a lie.

Here's the one that's giving me paws right now:

> What's greater than God.
>
> More evil than the devil.
>
> The poor have it.
>
> The rich need it.
>
> If you eat it, you'll die.

Absolutely nothing comes to mind.

Maybe I'm having trouble because I know next to nothing about God (I *know* Him without *knowing* Him), the devil (one guy I never want to meet!), being poor (I have more money than I could ever need) or being rich (I have less money than many but more than most).

Notice I didn't include eating. I know a lot about that. And I'd like to know more.

Or maybe I've simply become a flea brain.

Anyhow, when you have nothing better to do, think about the riddle. I'm like a dog with a bone when I get hold of a stumper, and I'd really like to bury this one and chew on some other challenge for a change.

Chapter 9.7
Believe in something bigger than yourself

I. What I learned from Dupe about believing in something bigger than yourself

Peanut and Tony display religious statues throughout their house, say grace before every meal, and wear scapular medals around their necks. A wooden crucifix hangs in a prominent spot on their living room wall, adorned with green fronds distributed on Palm Sunday at Most Precious Blood Roman Catholic Church.

That's where they to go Mass – on Sundays, holy days of obligation, special feast days and other occasions when they feel the need for extra prayer or reflection.

I asked Dupe why he often stopped by St. John's to put money in the metal collection box, but never attended services.

"I stay pretty much in constant contact with God," he replied. "Why save the conversation for a particular building on a particular day, when I can talk and listen to the Almighty wherever I am, whenever I get the urge?

"Designating a certain time and place to give honor and express thanks just doesn't fit with my communication style, son. Besides, some of the most pious people who sit in pews and sing hymns at the top of their lungs every Sunday are so full of judgment and hate, they'd find fault with Jesus Christ himself.

"For me, a park full of kids playing or a field covered with wildflowers is every bit as holy as a church is. So that's where I do my worshiping. One-on-one. On Sunday and every other day of the week."

Dupe talked to and about God a lot, so I knew he was a strong believer. As for attending church, I guess you couldn't really expect a guy without a bed or even a roof over his head to follow religious convention.

Personally, I enjoy going to services and I'm . . . well, I'm *faithful* about regular attendance. Every Saturday or Sunday you'll find me in some kind of house of worship, thanking God that I lost my CANN, got stuck in Newark, and have a happy life full of wonderful friends.

Two years ago I took Rite of Christian Initiation for Adults classes at St. John's and was confirmed a Catholic. In fact, now I'm an Extraordinary Minister of the Eucharistic and a Sacred Scripture Reader. Phil is, too. When I'm in town, we usually go to early Mass together every day.

But I've also attended Mormon and Buddhist temples; Jewish synagogues; Episcopalian, Presbyterian, Methodist, Lutheran and Baptist churches; Muslim mosques; Quaker meeting houses; Jehovah's Witnesses Kingdom Halls; Shinto shrines; and Anglican chapels. I've even been to services in bars, barns, basements, and bookstores.

Different religions have different beliefs and customs and practices, but the sense of

Speaking of music

Until I came to Earth, all I needed to survive was air, water and food. Nowadays, I could *survive* without music but, like Dupe, I couldn't *LIVE* without it (or bowling or friends). Here are a few of my favorites: rock 'n' roll band – Rolling Stones; country western singers – George Jones and Patsy Cline; operatic aria – *La Vergine degli Angeli* by Leontyne Price; movie score – *Jaws*; jazz vocalist – Ella Fitzgerald; rap song – Eminem's *Mockingbird*; hymn – *Christ the Lord is Risen Today*; jazz pianist – Thelonious Monk; metal band – AC/DC; Latin pop artist – Gloria Estefan. And, in my opinion, the three greatest entertainers of all time are Elvis Presley, Frank Sinatra and Michael Jackson. Michael's performance of *Billie Jean* on the 1983 Motown 25 TV special is an absolute *thriller*. Dupe wishes he had never shown me the video because afterward, moonwalking became my favorite mode of travel. Thank you, mirror neurons.

gratitude and peace I feel when I'm in any place of worship is the same.

It's definitely a new experience, though.

Paladinos don't believe in any kind of Supreme Being. What I'm about to tell you is going to sound really strange, even coming from me: Most Paladinos don't believe in life. They think we're all characters in a giant computer simulation.

I can't prove them wrong. I only know that when I fasten my sandals too tightly across my gills, it hurts. To the best of my knowledge, not even the nerdiest geek can code pain into a computer program. But I don't keep up with technology as well as some Paladinos do.

Dupe is one of the most rational, logical people I know, so at first I couldn't understand how he could accept an idea on faith alone.

"Somebody put us here, son, and just because we can't *see* who did it doesn't mean there's no one to see," he explained. "Call him God. Allah. Yahweh. Vishnu. Shakti. Call him Jim. Call him a her. The name doesn't matter. But someone, or something, is out there. Somewhere.

"Carl Sagan said the universe is governed by physical laws alone. But he was wrong. Physical laws create order. Only a higher power can create beauty. And this is a mighty beautiful world.

"Besides, any astronomer who spends his career trying to communicate with extraterrestrials has to be at least one electron short of a full shell. Even if they exist, and I'm not saying they don't, why on Earth would they want to talk to us?"

I decided to assume it was a rhetorical question. Otherwise, I'd have to answer honestly.

And then I wouldn't have a prayer of escaping detection.

There's so much sameness on Paladin, it was easy for me to believe that life was the result of a random physical event. But Earth is a planet of differences – in humans and geography and climate and language and so many other dimensions.

Earth is also a planet of passionate people.

Maybe science can – and did – create differences in the touchable, tangible aspects of our existence. Even if that's true, I'm now certain that science can't create love.

If it could, Paladin would be crawling with Casanovas and Mother Teresas.

Love doesn't come out of a test tube or a computer program or a collision of atoms. It comes from the heart of a loving creator.

That's what I believe. And, thank God, I believe it with all *my* heart.

II. What I learned on the job about believing in something bigger than yourself

Theoretically, hiring me as a cook at the Sunrise Senior Living Center in Kane, Pennsylvania, would be like hiring someone with a shoe fetish to work at Zappo's.

The temptation would be irresistible.

Eating is one of my favorite pastimes. I'm very, very good at it.

But my taste buds had been spoiled by Peanut and Mighty Minnie. Those women are to a kitchen what Mozart is to an orchestra. Gifted impresarios.

Don't get me wrong. The food at Sunrise isn't just edible; it's appetizing. But Peanut's and Mighty's culinary creations are divine. Exquisite. Savory and scrumptious. Luscious. Gratifying.

I won't go on. Although I could.

The fare at Sunrise was tailored to people whose digestive systems – and teeth – required soft, plain food. Nothing fancy. Just protein, vegetables and rice or potatoes.

Three times a day, residents who were physically able came to the dining room for their meals. Some preferred to eat cafeteria-style. Others wanted to be served at their tables.

Every morning for breakfast, and every evening for dinner, a man dressed in a starched and pressed Air Force uniform came through the line. At lunch time, the uniform was replaced by khaki pants, a white button-down shirt, and loafers.

Without fail, he instructed me to serve him "just half a scoop, half a scoop only, please" of each item on the menu.

"Discipline," he said emphatically each time I handed him his plate. "That's what the people in this country need. More discipline. Millions

of dollars spent every year on diets and they might as well flush it down the toilet. All anybody needs is a little self-control and willpower."

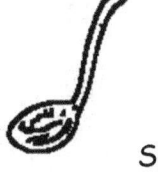

Soup ladle
by Dr. J.J.

One day after lunch, I asked Josie Kate, one of my fellow cooks, the reason behind the man's unusual dress code.

"You mean the Colonel?" she replied. "I can tell you the answer, but you ought to see for yourself. Meet me in the courtyard at 4:59 this afternoon and you'll find out. And I do mean 4:59."

I was there at the appointed time and had no sooner arrived when the bugled strains of "Taps" drifted out of a nearby window.

The Colonel appeared in a doorway, wearing his uniform. He walked to the pole in the middle of the courtyard and saluted the American flag that flew there.

After the recording of "Taps" ended, he slowly and methodically lowered the flag. He folded it, tucked it under his arm, clicked his heels together and turned back in the direction from which he had come.

"He's 85 years old, and is out here in his uniform every morning at 7:30 sharp," Josie said. "As soon as 'Reveille' has played, he sends the flag up the pole. Every afternoon at 5 o'clock sharp, just like you saw him, he's back to take it down. Rain, snow, pneumonia, flu . . . nothing stops him.

"He says raising and lowering the flag is his way of honoring our country. He always tells me, 'It's not as great as it could be, Josie, and it's not as great as it once was, but there's still no place like it on Earth'."

I was surprised he didn't tell Josie there was no place like it in the cosmos. But he probably hasn't visited any other solar systems, so how would he know?

I've traveled extensively, of course. Not to every planet in every galaxy in every universe in existence, though. So I myself can't say there's no place like the United States.

But Colonel Edwin B. James' unflagging faith in his country gave me food for thought.

He was talking about the United States not as a geographic location, but as a home to people with similar values, beliefs, customs and personality traits that were manifested in the endeavors and achievements of Americans, past, present and to come.

Land of the free; home of the brave.

He believed in his country because he believed in its people, whose actions and accomplishments are often based on ideals that transcend time and place and person.

That isn't true of Paladinos. We don't have underlying motivations. We just do as we're instructed and don't ask questions.

But here, earthlings across the planet – not just in the U.S. – cherish principles such as freedom, equality, justice and democracy that give them hope and energy and an abiding sense of purpose.

If you had told me 10 years ago that I'd understand the importance of ideals, I probably would have looked at you cross-eyed. I couldn't have comprehended ideals as a concept, let alone appreciated their significance in life.

But then one Sunday night it snowed eight inches in Newark. And when the alarm went off at 6:30 on Monday morning, even though I was tempted to pull the covers up to my chin and stay in my nice warm bed, I got up and went to work at a photo processing lab.

Not because I would have been fired if I hadn't. Leaving jobs is, after all, a regular part of my job.

Not because I loved the work. The nasty odor of developer, stop bath and fixer chemicals permeated my clothes and made me queasy.

And not because I needed the money. Although the lab paid me only minimum wage, the newspaper gave me a full salary plus benefits.

You might be thinking, "What's the big deal? I would have gotten up and gone to work, too."

In which case the explanation would be that it's simply human nature. Except that, technically/scientifically/biologically, I'm not human.

I'm not a philosopher, either. But I think the reason I shed my flannel pajamas, donned a smelly white lab coat and trudged out into the snow is that my immediate comfort and welfare aren't as important nowadays as keeping my word and following through on my commitments are.

Personal responsibility makes sense to me now.

It's like bringing a covered dish to a Baptist Church picnic. You wouldn't be breaking any kind of law if you showed up empty-handed, but it just wouldn't be polite or neighborly.

Believe me: You can never go wrong by doing the right thing.

Chapter 9.8
Exercise your free will

I. What I learned from Dupe about exercising your free will

Dupe lettered in varsity football, baseball and basketball in high school. He also graduated as valedictorian of his senior class. He could have gone to any one of six different colleges on athletic or academic scholarships.

He chose not to go anywhere except across the Hudson River.

And I emphasize the word "chose."

"People use the phrase 'have to' way too often, son," Dupe said to me once during a conversation about a socialite who faked her own kidnapping to avoid getting married.

"'I can't stay to watch the game because I have to be at work early tomorrow.' Or 'I have to go to my aunt's house for Thanksgiving dinner.' Or 'I have to buy a gift for my wife's birthday.'

Ear of corn
by Dr. J.J.

"The way they talk, you'd think someone was holding a gun to their head. There's nothing in the world we have to do except die. Paying taxes included. We do things because we want to do them, or because we want to avoid the consequences of not doing them.

"Either way, it's our decision. Once we recognize the fact that we always have options, it's easier for us to live with the choices we make."

Paladin offered what you might call a no-alternative lifestyle. So I couldn't identify with what Dupe was saying based on my experiences there.

But life on Earth is a different matter. Nobody tells me what to do or makes decisions for me. I can do anything I want and nothing I don't.

Some people might not have enjoyed helping Angie pick and shuck 300 ears of corn, but I did. On Paladin food is manufactured or grown hydroponically in 130-story buildings, so I'd never before visited a farm.

Each time I pulled the thick green leaves and golden silk off a cob, I was amazed at the sight of row after row of plump, lemon-yellow kernels.

Real. Fresh. Straight from the earth.

When Jimmy built a patio off his kitchen, I spent hours with him at a nearby rock quarry, picking out stones and piling them into the bed of a rental truck. Once we got to his house, we put the stones in wheelbarrows, carted them around back, and stacked them in neat piles.

We worked from 7 o'clock on a Saturday morning till 9 o'clock that night, hefting and toting four loads of stones that weighed eight to 15 pounds apiece. Jimmy cursed and complained all day long and asked why I didn't do the same. I told him I was having fun getting exercise without exercising. And it was the truth (of course!).

I washed the stained-glass windows at St. John's, poking my index finger into a white cotton t-shirt square so I could remove stubborn bits of dirt and grime from each small, lead-framed piece. For eight days I climbed the ladder, rinsed the windows to loosen debris, sprayed the glass with special cleaner, and polished every single tiny pane.

Father Mo didn't ask me to do it. In fact, he asked me not to. He said the tedium of the task would try the patience of Job. But because I was surrounded by the vibrant colors that Paladinos love, I actually found the project pleasurable. Father Mo made the sign of the cross when I told him so.

Bagging litter along five miles of interstate, cleaning 90 years of accumulated junk from the un-air-conditioned attic of the local community center during a heat wave, re-staining 10 sets of patio furniture from Phil's rental houses – I've spent lots of time doing lots of things that lots of people would find burdensome.

So far I've enjoyed everything I've done. But I don't know whether that's because I only do what I like, or because I like whatever I do.

Take your pick.

I'll be happy either way.

II. What I learned on the job about exercising your free will

As the Academic Computing Specialist (ACS) for the environmental science department at the Alaska Pacific University in Anchorage, Alaska, I was in my element.

Not element as in Mendeleyev's periodic table. Element as in milieu.

When I daydream, I imagine myself as the swarthy Captain Nemo, piloting his cutting-edge submarine, Nautilus, in search of a mysterious sea monster *Twenty Thousand Leagues Under the Sea.*

Water. Travel. Technology. What a tantalizing trifecta.

But I digress . . . . .

High heel shoe
by Dr. J.J.

At the university, I was in my technological milieu.

According to the job description for the ACS position, I was responsible for "managing the installation, configuration, upgrading and maintenance of hardware and software used by faculty, as well as providing day-to-day technical support for academic computer operations."

In English: I supported the computer-related work of professors.

My favorite was Carson Spring. She was a world-renown authority on chemical contaminants in waterfowl.

She was also six feet tall without her shoes, had long blond hair she kept in a ponytail, and wore skirts that were shorter than a list of Hollywood conservatives.

The day after she returned from testifying before the Environmental Protection Agency on mercury concentration in Black Scoters, I walked into her office to find her filling cardboard boxes with books.

"Do you want to dance?" she asked me. "Because I do. Give me your hand. Let's jitterbug right here, right now."

I didn't have time to wonder why she suddenly wanted to jump and jive. All I could think about was that she was very tall. She wore very high heels. And she wanted to get very close to my feet.

I couldn't let that happen to my gills.

So I grabbed a heavy volume off a shelf, passed it to her, and asked what she was doing.

> ### Speaking of home
>
> You might expect someone from outer space to favor sleek, metal, angular furnishings similar to what the Jetsons had in their Skypad Apartment in Orbit City. But my taste runs to European antiques. My living room, which Phil says is elegant but cozy, includes an eight-foot English Chippendale sofa that's Dupe's favorite reading spot, two Louis XVI marquetry side tables, a Spanish vargueno that serves as my writing desk, and a pair of Italian Savanarola curule chairs with thick, tasseled velvet cushions and matching stools. A marble-top, parcel gilt console is between them. Mama Rosa often nods off in one of the chairs, feet up on a stool and empty sherry glass in her hand. In my home, the living room is for living, not looking.

"I'm leaving the nest. Finally flying the proverbial coop," she said. "I was scheduled to start a sabbatical, but I submitted my resignation. I'm not coming back next year. Or ever.

"I've done all I can do for the birds. I've done all I can do for the students and the department. Now it's time to do something for myself."

Dr. Carson Spring, popular professor, sought-after media figure, author of three books and more than 70 journal articles, was leaving Alaska for Florida.

She was trading snow for sunshine, academics for art, and the classroom for a Key West cottage.

"I used to get energy from teaching and research," she said. "It was invigorating and stimulating. But a while ago, my work became work.

"All the energy was going out. None was coming back in. And try as I might, I couldn't change my feelings.

"So I'm changing my life instead. I've always enjoyed sculpting, but never had enough time to pursue it. Now I will.

"I bought a little place with a studio that's full of windows and sunlight. I feel revived just thinking about it.

"I've already decided on my first subject. And it won't be a bird. It will be a bust of an old conch fisherman I met in Mallory Square last spring. He has a face with more angles than an icosahedron and eyes more penetrating than Picasso's.

"It will be just the kind of project I need to stop working with my head and start working with my hands.

"*And* with my heart."

If Carson lived on Paladin, the COPS would never let her leave the university. But on Earth, she could carve out exactly the kind of life she wanted for herself.

Of course she wanted to dance. Why, I almost broke into an Irish jig myself.

It makes me happy to see others make happy choices.

On Paladin, all of our assignments are for life, without the possibility of personal preference, pardon, or parole. On Earth, there are so many options, it doesn't make sense to be miserable or discontented

Right now you're probably thinking, "Easy for him to say. He has no spouse. No children. No ailing parents. No mortgage. No college educations to finance. No pet. No one who's depending on him for anything at all."

And you'd be right.

But I'm pretty sure that if I did, my family and the responsibilities that came with it would give me the why and the will to live. If I didn't like my job, I'd either quit and find a new one, or I'd start thinking in terms of everything my job made possible for my family.

I'd change my circumstances or change my attitude.

Earthlings sometimes *get* where they are by chance, which is a foreign concept to Paladinos. But they often *stay* where they are by choice.

As someone who moved from one solar system to another, I know better than most people that change isn't always easy. But in most places on your planet, it's always possible.

Chapter 9.9
Take care of your health

I. What I learned from Dupe about taking care of your health

Dupe doesn't *get* up from naps; he *pushes* up or *sits* up.

He'll wake from a sound slumber in the corner of an alley, roll onto his stomach, and start doing push-ups. Two hundred. One hundred. Fifty. Never fewer than 25.

Or he'll roll onto his back and start doing sit-ups. Three hundred. Two hundred. One hundred. Never fewer than 50.

Before he begins reading on his daily visits to the Newark Public Library, he heads to the basement, hangs from a cold-water plumbing pipe, and does 20 pull-ups. He does another 20 before he leaves.

One day, when I decided to pay attention, I counted 300 push-ups, 400 sit-ups and 50 pull-ups.

Because of my mirror neurons, I almost felt sore after watching him.

"Would you go an entire day without brushing your teeth, son?" he asked me when I inquired about his regimen. "Of course not. And neither would anyone else who had a choice. So why would anyone go an entire day without exercise?

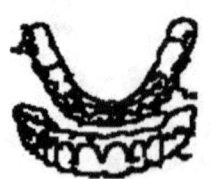

Dentures
by Dr. J.J.

"If your teeth fall out, you can get a set of dentures. Nicer than the ones God gave you. But you can't replace your body. It's the only one you'll ever get, so you have to take care of it.

"Some people pay a lot of money to join gyms. That's fine. But it isn't necessary. Just walk when you could ride. Run when you could walk. And push, sit and pull yourself up every chance you get.

"If you do that, plus cut out junk food and cut down on portion size, I guarantee you'll feel like your body's your friend, not your enemy."

I asked Dupe why, if it were really that obvious, obesity and poor health were the norm, rather than the exception.

"There's a big difference between theory and implementation, son," he said. "Just because an idea's simple to understand doesn't mean it's easy to do. The wheel is one of the simplest ideas imaginable. But it took almost 7,000 years before it was invented.

"Stroll through the self-help section in any bookstore and you'll see what I mean. All those authors are making millions of dollars selling straightforward solutions to problems that the average person finds overwhelming.

"But to break a bad habit, like overeating or inactivity, you need to do more than read. You have to move something besides your eyes."

Dupe has a talent for reducing explanations to their most basic truths: Good health is the result of actions, not intentions.

I doubt that even a KISSeR enforcement agent could find any fat to trim off that statement.

Dupe's right about the importance of good health. In the journey of life, our bodies are our transportation. We can sail through on a yacht, or chug along on a tugboat.

I have to admit, I've always been more of a chugger than a sailor. Most Paladinos are.

Our life expectancy is a pre-programmed certainty. We don't know when we'll die, but the government does. When the time comes, *pfffft*. One nanosecond here; the next, gone.

Because the quality of our health doesn't factor into the quantity of our years, we don't pay much attention to our physical condition. Even if it makes us sick.

Or keeps us stuck.

For example, I knew a Paladino who ate so many rondononios from the planet Finbilaptinaptian, he gained more than 800 pounds and had to quit traveling.

The problem wasn't that his CANN was too small. The problem was that scientists couldn't develop a remote activator button with enough neural neutralizing charge to vaporize him. So he was trapped on Paladin, relegated to eating local food or treats he paid neighbors to bring him from other planets.

Being homebound 24/7 is what I would call a very narrow existence. My advice to him would have been: Shape up. It won't affect the length of your life, but it could definitely affect the breadth.

I've noticed that some earthlings act like Paladinos when it comes to taking care of their health. They end up with bodies that work against them, rather than for them.

The opinion of an ex-extraterrestrial probably doesn't carry much weight, but I believe all the medical experts who say that, for most people, a combination of regular conditioning and proper nutrition can change their lives.

Quality- *and* length-wise.

I think I'll give it a try myself. I've already cut out cigars and tapered almost completely off the bourbon. Maybe I should also scale down on the sugar and beef up my workout routine.

Even if I don't gain any time on my life expectancy clock, I have absolutely nothing to lose.

Except maybe a few extra Henry's cheesecake pounds.

II. What I learned on the job about taking care of your health

The tallest building in Little Rock, Arkansas, is the Metropolitan National Bank Tower.

Forty stories might not seem like many compared to 108 at the Sears Tower or 102 at the Empire State Building. But if you run up the Metropolitan's 888 stairs three times a week, I guarantee you'll think it's a high number.

That's what Chris Hedgewood did every Monday, Wednesday and Friday on his way home from the office.

We bumped into one another when I was working in the building's maintenance department. Literally.

I was replacing an anti-slip tread on the 20th-floor landing when Chris came barreling around the corner. He wasn't expecting to see me, and I certainly wasn't expecting to see him. Nobody took the stairs in the building, even when they were only going up a couple of flights. Or down a single floor.

Chris crashed into me. Knocked me over. And nearly fell on my gills.

I have to admit that I yelled a few choice Paladino cuss words. I couldn't help it. My vocal chords always loosen up in warning in direct proportion to the degree my gills shrink up in fear.

Luckily, Chris had no idea what I was saying.

When I got my wits about me, I asked him a question Dupe had put to me on the day I tripped over him in the alley. What in Sam Hill and blue blazes did he think he was doing?

I must have looked pretty upset, because he apologized profusely and offered to buy me a cup of coffee.

After the shock he gave me, I really could have used a shot of bourbon. But my shift wasn't over, so I settled for caffeine.

Coffee mug
by Dr. J.J.

When we sat down in the café, he asked whether I'd heard of the Arkansas Respiratory Health Association.

I told him I hadn't. Until I got the job assignment, I hadn't even heard of Arkansas.

He said he was executive director of the organization, which worked to prevent lung disease and offered support to people afflicted with it. He ran the stairs three days a week to keep in shape and demonstrate the importance of pulmonary and cardiovascular conditioning.

"Too many people are like Oscar Madison in *The Odd Couple*," he said. "They think good health 'just comes' with life, like gravy with meat. But they're wrong. We're no different than a car or a sewing machine. We need proper maintenance and care in order to function properly."

He began to inhale in huge gulps and exhale in loud bursts.

"Ahhhh," he said as he sucked in oxygen. "Whoooo," he said as he blew it out.

"Ahhhh." "Whoooo." "Ahhhh." "Whoooo."

Three times in a row. Which, as far as I was concerned, was at least two times too many.

"Just like a fireplace bellow. You ought to try it," he suggested.

Ironic, don't you think? There he was, encouraging someone with a pair of gills to breathe deeply.

Why, if I'd had a bucket of water for my feet, I could have taken in enough oxygen at that very moment to create a vacuum in the room.

But that would have been scarier for him than the end of *Carrie*, when Sissy Spacek's bloody hand reached out of the grave to grab her best friend's arm.

And very dangerous for me.

People don't mind having their breath taken away by beauty. But when a man dressed in a maintenance uniform does it after first removing his sandals and socks, they're bound to get upset.

So I didn't say a word. I let him keep right on talking.

"There's a reason we use the term 'breathe easier' when we feel relieved or free of restraints. Being able to take a good, deep breath makes you want to beat your fists against your chest like Tarzan. He stayed fit by swinging around in the jungle. We don't have vines here in Little Rock, but we can run and walk and climb. And speaking of climbing . . . ."

He then tried to recruit me for a "Power Up the Tower" stair-climbing event the association was organizing at the Metropolitan to raise money for lung disease research and education.

I've noticed that people affiliated with non-profits see everyone they meet as a potential donor or volunteer. But he took the concept of persistent persuasion to new heights.

By the time we finished our coffee, I had given him $150 and agreed to man the registration desk at the fundraiser.

I'm not claiming that sitting at a table passing out forms will help you start an exercise program. But for me, at least, it was a step in the right direction.

I signed up for a Zumba class that Mrs. Rosenblatt said would give me an intense workout. I'd actually call it an intense playout.

Fitness is fun!

So far I've lost seven pounds and gained lots of new friends. I've also received lunch and dinner invitations from four very attractive women.

Being the only male in the room is a real benefit.

So is having mirror neurons. After watching a DVD of Beto Perez just once, I delivered a performance in class that had everyone, including the instructor, zooming over to my side to *ooh* and *aah*.

In my opinion, if you want to get your body and your social life in shape, Zumba can't be beat.

Chapter 9.10
Eat sardines!

What I learned on my own about enjoying simple pleasures

I know a man whose idea of a perfect appetizer is Bugles corn horns dipped in a combination of ketchup and sour cream with a dash of pepper.

I know a woman who keeps a jar of pig's knuckles in her refrigerator for snacking between meals.

And I know a 75 – year – old grandfather who can't buy more than one box of peanut butter Cap'n Crunch cereal at a time because he'll eat them all in one sitting.

Speaking of snacks

Lots of earthlings think a day isn't complete without sugar – cake, candy or cookies that send an "I'm satisfied" signal to their brains. Me? I have a swalty tooth. I love cheesecake, but my general preference is for sweet and salty flavor combinations. A fat kernel of popcorn wrapped in a smushed and stretched Milk Dud is tough to beat, especially when watching a good comedy such as *The Thing*, *E.T.*, or *Alien*. I also like to dip Wendy's fries in a Frosty or use Ruffles potato chips to eat soft ice cream. My swalty cravings started after I tasted prosciutto-wrapped cantaloupe. Now I add a pinch of salt to moistened jelly beans and make Chex Mix with Tony Chacere's Creole Seasoning and cinnamon brown sugar. If you're thinking New Jersey = salt water taffy = swalty, know this: The colorful Atlantic City confection doesn't contain salt water. Legend has it that a storm flooded a candy store, soaking through everything on the shelves and prompting the owner to rename his saturated product "salt water taffy." I'm not sure about the story, but if you have a swalty tooth, you'd better bring your own shaker to the Boardwalk.

Me? I like sardines. Right out of the tin. With plenty of old-fashioned yellow mustard.

I eat them at least twice a day. I prefer the cans with a key attached to the side, but those are hard to find. So I generally buy pull-tabs.

Tin of sardines
by Dr. J.J.

When Dupe introduced me to the palate-pleasing satisfaction of sardines, he told me the fish are rich in long-chain omega-3 fatty acids.

Apparently they reduce coronary artery disease, cut the risk of heart attack and stroke, ease rheumatoid arthritis pain, and fight depression and anxiety.

I don't have any of those problems. I eat them because they taste good.

I'd rather have seven sardines packed in oil and slathered with mustard than a banana split topped with chocolate sauce, whipped cream and a maraschino cherry.

Everyone should have a favorite food. I'll bet that if you tried a tin, yours would be sardines.

But whatever it is, don't save it for last. You might not have room.

The best things in life should always come first!

Be happy you're a human being.

Be happy.
You're a human being.

Living

Chapter 10
Feet of daring: my last job as an undocumented alien

It had been raining non-stop for five days. The gutters were overflowing, puddles looked like small lakes, and even gas stations were selling umbrellas.

My gills had never been happier.

I was crossing the "Trenton Makes" Bridge over the Delaware River and heading into Morrisville, where I was going to spend a couple of weeks as a front desk clerk at the Holiday Inn Express. Suddenly, the driver in the car 30 yards or so ahead of me pulled to the right as far as possible and turned off the engine.

A woman got out, cell phone in hand, and ran to the other side of the bridge. As she did, I noticed that a section of the guardrail had been torn away.

When I stopped my car and followed her, I saw the river's swollen current battering an almost completely submerged school bus caught on an outcropping of rocks. Screaming children were everywhere, waving at passersby with one hand and holding on to anything close with the other.

I heard the woman with the cell phone call for a rescue squad.

"And send a helicopter and a scuba team, too" she pleaded.

But I knew that, by the time help arrived, it would be too late.

I kicked off my sandals and jumped.

My gills surged as I swam toward the children, five by my count.

The right panel of the bus' rear door had broken free on impact and was floating away. I grabbed it, dragged it across the water, and wedged it between several large rocks.

Then, one by one, I retrieved the little ones – none of whom could have been older than six or seven – and placed them atop the door.

"Mrs. Brothers, Mrs. Brothers and Jackie," one of them cried. "They're still on the bus. Please. Please. You have to get Mrs. Brothers and Jackie."

I tore deep into the river and looked for the bus driver and the remaining child.

No one.

I dived again and searched the portion of the bus that was underwater. Nothing.

One more time.

Empty.

I turned toward the children on the rocks, who were all pointing frantically to a spot down the river.

A woman had one of her arms hooked around the trunk of a small tree sticking out of the water and the other around the waist of a child. She didn't look as if she could hold on much longer.

I swam over, put Jackie on my back and told her to hang on to my neck. I pulled Mrs. Brothers to my side and told her not to do anything except keep her head above water.

The current roared in our ears as I swam back to the rocks.

When we arrived, three men were pulling children off the door and onto the deck of a boat. They were all crying, but one little girl with curly blond hair was especially upset.

"Teddy. What about Teddy?" she sobbed. "He doesn't know how to swim. He'll drown if you don't save him."

Mrs. Brothers, the bus driver, looked at me and shook her head.

"Teddy's a stuffed animal, not a person. Jessica takes him to school every day."

Her words made the little girl sob even harder.

I dived into the water again.

Backpacks, lunchboxes, sodden grammar books, toys and even a skateboard were in a heap at the lowest point of the bus, under the steering wheel and dashboard. But no Teddy.

I checked in and around every seat. No Teddy.

Then I spotted him, hanging upside down in the water. The yellow ribbon around his neck was snagged on a piece of metal from a window frame.

I pulled the stuffed bear loose and started to swim to the surface.

As I did, I glanced again at the heap: an orange sweatshirt, multi-hued rubber snake, navy blue and red lunchbox, green skateboard, pink purse, purple backpack.

Teddy
by Dr. J.J

Remember when I told you that Paladinos are very color-sensitive?

I saw Mrs. Brothers' jacket crammed between the back of her seat and its frame. I tugged it free, zipped it up, and cinched the ties around the hood to create a makeshift sack.

Once I had stuffed it full of the rainbow of items, I headed upward, skateboard under my right arm.

When my shoulders broke the surface, I heard a roar that was distinct from the sound of the rushing water.

The bridge was lined with people, all of whom were cheering and clapping and waving. And they all seemed to be looking at me. Car horns began to blare, a nearby skiff sounded a bell, and a general cacophony arose to accompany my emergence from the depths.

What on Earth was going on?

Suddenly, a helicopter with a ladder suspended from its belly appeared out of nowhere and a man in a scuba suit climbed down. Before I had a chance to protest, he clipped a vest around my chest and waved to someone above.

I could feel myself rising out of the water and into the sky. I looked down at the scene below and . . . .

Holy mackerel!

Jumping Jehosaphat!

Snakes, snails and puppy dog tails!

My socks were gone and my gills were fluttering in the breeze!

Chapter 11
Two feet away from dissection and death

You know part of what happened next, but not all.

What you know is that the people were cheering because I was *alive*.

The cars parked on the bridge had attracted more cars, and each time a driver or a passenger got out to look or offer help, the woman with the cell phone told them I had jumped in the river.

Everyone watched me rescue the children, retrieve Mrs. Brothers and Jackie, then dive into the water again.

Everyone waited . . . and waited . . . and waited . . . for me to come back up.

When I didn't resurface, fearful whispers passed up and down the row of onlookers.

"Where is he?"

"There must be more kids down there."

"No one can survive under water that long."

"Oh, dear God."

When rescue units arrived, they were told that I had gone down to look for more children and hadn't been seen again. The helicopter scuba crew expected to find at least one dead body in the wreckage of the bus. Instead, they found me.

Shoeless, sockless, but very much alive.

Here's the part you don't know but probably figured out:

My stirring gills created quite a stir.

The paramedics who pulled me into the helicopter didn't notice. They were too busy.

As they wrapped layers of blankets around me, divers dropped into the river to make sure I was correct that everyone on the bus was safe and sound. Then the helicopter took me to Newark-Wayne Hospital.

I knew that the landing on the hospital helipad would be my last touchdown on Earth. Once the physicians and nurses saw my feet, I'd never be able to go back to Paladin. I'd never even be able to go back to my home in Newark.

I'd soon be taken to a new home. My permanent place of residence.

A life sciences lab.

Only for me, it would be a death sciences lab.

I pushed the blankets below my knees and wrapped them as tightly as I could around my ankles.

When we landed, we were greeted by a host of white- and blue-coated medical personnel who strapped me onto a gurney and whisked me into an elevator.

As I was wheeled into an examining room, I spotted a horde of media at the end of the hall. I heard someone say a representative of Ripley's Believe It or Not! was there, too.

All of them wanted to talk to the hero with superhuman lungs who had rescued the stranded schoolchildren – and their treasures – from the river.

A hero with superhuman lungs?

How about an ex-alien with normal Paladino gills?

The emergency room staff was preparing to treat me for exposure, but it wasn't the elements that had sent me into a state of shock.

It was pure, unadulterated, mind-numbing, bone-chilling dread.

I had been on Earth for six years, living as an earthling. I had traveled to hundreds of places and met thousands of people, all of whom knew me as Dr. J.J.

I *was* Dr. J.J.

I wanted to go on being Dr. J.J.

I wanted to go on being. Period.

When the truth was discovered, appreciation would turn into astonishment. Aversion would be next, followed by abhorrence, which would culminate in extensive anxiety and enormous alarm.

But it had to happen.

And it did.

Chapter 11.5
Feet first

These are the words I yelled as I tried to swing my legs off the gurney and stand up:

Kfjeodjsnv! Brdksowurnclakdn-dkpwienv!! Mkdliwqlsma!!!

Fljesx!!!!

Ycvmii!!!!!

I forgot my manners. And my English.

These are the words the people in the examining room yelled as the blankets around my feet slid to the floor and my gills were exposed:

Je*** Chr***!!

What the h***!!

Holy sh**!!

This is what Dr. Harper Bates yelled when curiosity-seekers poured into the small space:

Clear the room!

Everyone out!

I mean *now*!

Dr. Bates told Nurse Dorothy Philipps to close the door to the room and pull the curtain so no one in the hallway could stare through the window. He began inspecting my gills with clinical curiosity, while she began inspecting my face with a look that was part terror, part tenderness.

Then the chief of staff of the hospital rushed through the door, accompanied by the chief residents in podiatry, surgery and psychiatry, the city police chief and the chief medical examiner.

The chief physicians wanted to put me through a battery of tests, the police chief wanted to put me in jail, and the chief medical examiner wanted to put my feet under a microscope . . . in little pieces.

Then representatives of the CIA, the FBI, the NIH, the CDC, and the DoD arrived.

Over the next two months I was checked up, checked over and checked out. Poked, probed, prodded and polygraphed. X-rayed, imaged and scanned. Inspected, investigated and interrogated.

While the government had me in what it called protective custody, professors, preachers, pundits, and publications called for my release. People from everywhere on the planet wanted to see and touch the hero with the funny-looking feet.

When the physicians finished their tests and the scientists finished their studies and the bureaucrats finished their questioning and the military leaders finished their background checks, the President of the United States held a press conference in the Rose Garden announcing that I would be released.

"The best minds in the world have determined that Mr. Jackalone poses no threat – physical, medical, biological or mental – to anyone, anywhere, and that there is no legal, ethical or moral basis for holding him against his will.

"He is anxious to return to his home in Newark, and I am pleased to report that he and I will fly there this afternoon on Air Force One.

"Dr. J.J. demonstrated uncommon valor, spirit and self-sacrifice when he jumped into the Delaware to rescue the children from Grand View Elementary School.

"When he leaves Washington today, he will take with him not only our country's highest civilian award for meritorious service, the Presidential Medal of Freedom, but also the admiration and affection of a grateful nation."

Medal
by Dr. J.J.

With that, he pinned the badge on my chest, shook my hand and gave me a solid hug. I returned his embrace, but gently.

Of course.

I didn't want the news cameras to catch the President waggling his shoes six inches off the freshly mown grass of the White House lawn.

Chapter 12
And they lived happily ever after

"And you know the rest, because here I am."

The moment I spoke those words, members of the TV studio audience jumped to their feet, clapping even louder than my teammates had on the day I bowled a perfect game.

Rand Goottin, host of "Talk of the Town," stood and grabbed my hand. He pulled me up from the couch and pumped my arm like he was trying to inflate a bicycle tire, grinning all the while.

I knew it wasn't my saga that made him look like a hungry man viewing a holiday ham. It was the ratings the broadcast would generate. In his mind, he was already deciding how to spend the bonus money he'd get when he re-negotiated his contract tomorrow.

Once I had returned to Newark from Washington, the anchors of every talk show on every station in every city in every country on the planet called to invite me on their programs. After being featured in a five-part series in the *Star-Ledger*, I decided to tell my tale live on Rand's show because he was a local personality and the first person to interview me when I began my Dr. J.J. column.

Dupe had been watching from the comfort and quiet of a small room behind stage. He walked out between the curtains, came over to my side and squeezed my right shoulder.

"You did a nice job, son. Sounded just like a natural-born storyteller."

I squeezed his shoulder in return and then gave him a full two-armed hug.

"Dupe, I'm sorry I never told you about all this till a few weeks ago. I should have, I know. You of all people deserved to know the truth

"I never had a buddy or a pal or a chum in my life until I met you. It took me 27 years and 12.5 million miles, but there's no doubt that I found the best friend in the universe.

"I wasn't afraid you'd think I was crazy. I knew you'd believe me, even if you were the only person on Earth who would. I just wanted to go to my grave without breathing a word about it to anyone.

"I don't feel like an alien anymore. I haven't for a long, long time. It's like you always say, some things just aren't relevant. A short while after I came here, being from another planet quit being relevant to me. I didn't think it would be relevant to you, either."

Dupe held up his hand and waved it from side to side. Just as he'd done on the day we met and on just about every other day we'd seen each other during the last six years.

"You're right, son. Knowing you're an alien doesn't change a thing. But I'd be lying if I said it wasn't interesting. Interesting in a completely useless sort of way, that is.

"Besides, I could tell pretty quick that there was something not quite right about you. Anybody who wears white socks and sandals when it's snowing outside has to be from outer space. Or from California. Either way, I was pretty much on the right track.

"Now come on. Let's get out of here. It's time for my nap."

And time for me to get back to normal life.

Back to life as a normal human being.

A normal human being who just happens to have gills on his feet.

Very, very smiley face
by Dr. J.J.

Epilogue

I know what you're thinking right now and what you've probably been thinking all along: I must have been stark raving out of my mind to leave my CANN behind in the first place.

Sure, the booze and tobacco were nice, but how could I jeopardize a lifetime of travel for a few fleeting seconds of gratification? How could I defy the scouts' teaching and risk being trapped on Earth forever?

Why did I think I was above The Rule?

I asked myself those very questions over and over after I lost my CANN. I contemplated, meditated, percolated and speculated. I ate the equivalent of 150 jrhkdibns. Like a true earthling, I lost sleep, weight and hair thinking about what I had done. Once I even sat in a bathtub full of ice in the hope that the freezing cold would shock my brain into understanding.

Morning, noon and night I wondered why I'd been such an idiot.

I'll tell you what I eventually concluded.

I hadn't been an idiot at all. I'd made the right choice back then, and I'd make it again if I had the chance. All that endless analyzing and scrutinizing, and it turned out the answer was floating around in my subconscious the whole time.

I left my CANN behind because, back then, smoking cigars and sipping bourbon every afternoon on my Paladin balcony brought me pleasure.

That's something we're ALL looking for.

Each and every single one of us – even a former alien like me – has to be able to count on something that gives us brief moments of happiness or, for the truly fortunate, lifelong joy.

It can be as simple as indulging in a quiet cup of morning coffee, as rewarding as rearing a child, as challenging as climbing the world's tallest mountains, as satisfying as helping a war veteran adjust to civilian life, or as exciting as watching a college basketball game go into double-overtime.

Whatever it is, we can't be content without it.

What I'm telling you isn't merely my opinion, it's a fact.

Paladinos are known for not giving advice unless they're absolutely certain their information is correct. It took months of head-scratching aggravation and downright mental torture before I knew the truth, but I know it now just as certainly as I know that chickens don't have lips.

Save yourself some trouble. Listen to me.

Don't sit around wishing your life were different. Figure out what makes you happy, then go find it. And don't let *anything* come between you and whatever it is.

Leave your can behind if you have to. I did.

Six years ago, I walked away from something I thought I needed more than anything else in the world. Just so I could enjoy a few earthly pleasures.

Look where it got me.

Right. Here. Stranded.

I lost my CANN and I've been flying high ever since.

I'm still searching for what I left behind on that vacant lot years ago. But not because I want to go home. No, Earth is my home now, and I never want to leave.

Speaking of happiness

Before you embark on a trans-galactic quest for happiness, let me tell you what I think is at the very heart of the matter: avoiding alienation, no pun intended. Flying solo is quick and convenient. Living solo is difficult and lonely. We all need a team of three best friends we can count on every day, in every way. 1.) Ourself. 2.) A true-blue pal of the likes of Dupe. 3.) God (or the equivalent). With that trio on our side, there isn't a person or problem in the world that can bring us down. Having a wife, husband or special someone in addition is like topping a warm-and-gooey fudge brownie with a scoop of vanilla ice cream. Nice, but, take it from me, not necessary for contentment. I have plenty more to say about happiness, particularly as it relates to being your own best friend. But as Dupe remarked when I met him, "That's another story. For another time."

I want to find my CANN because I want to donate it to science. Maybe the brains at NASA or MIT or Cal Tech will be able to replicate it. Then an American manufacturer can make a gazillion just like it and stores can sell them to anyone and everyone who wants to zip through space like I once did.

You see, the ability to be happy is what most sets humans apart from other creatures in the cosmos.

Happiness is possible because humans have the power to make choices in life. Whom to love and what to do and why to do it and whether to think and how to behave.

But happiness can sometimes be elusive, because it seeks out few people. Most of us have to seek out happiness for ourselves.

Sometimes it's sitting right in front of us in the middle of the living room and we just have to open our eyes to see it. But we often have to go to great lengths to find it. And I mean that quite literally.

If you can't find happiness where you are, you need to look somewhere else.

Even if it's in outer space.

A CANN can help you get there.

So my advice to you is: If you're ever shopping at Walmart and see a display of travel CANNs in the checkout lane, grab one.

Grab one and *GO*!

CANN of corn
by Dr. J.J.

I promise it will be worth the trip.

Post-epilogue
What's next?

Well, that sums up 257 pages of my notes. I have 14,894 more in 75 different journals. They're filled from cover to cover with sketches, stories, reflections and recollections of my experiences on Earth.

Life here is so interesting, I could write a book.

Maybe I will.

Such as:

A Traveler's Guide to Cooking: What six years spent eating around the world taught me about meal preparation.

Perhaps:

A Traveler's Guide to Customer Service: What six years spent in retail positions taught me about sales support.

Or:

A Traveler's Guide to Masculinity: What six years spent observing alpha males taught me about being a man.

How about:

A Traveler's Guide to Happiness: What six years spent as a lucky human being taught me about contentment.

Possibly:

A Traveler's Guide to Common Courtesy: What six years spent interacting with earthlings taught me about being polite.

Eventually, I might write them all.

If I hadn't been born on Paladin, I could steal a phrase from the movie screen and say, "Coming Soon."

But a Paladino, even one who's now a full-blooded earthling, can't make a promise he doesn't intend to keep.

So although I might write something, or I might write everything, I can't say for sure that I'll write anything.

What do you think I should do? I'd appreciate your opinion.

You can contact me at atravelersguidetoliving.com.

I hope to hear from you!

www.ingramcontent.com/pod-product-compliance
Lightning Source LLC
Chambersburg PA
CBHW071256130626

46556CB00003B/1345